Deadly Secrets

A Meadowood Mystery

Nancy M. Wade

Also By: Nancy M. Wade

A Meadowood Mystery – series

Scarecrows and Corpses

Reunion With Death

Deadly Bones

Berry Little Murder

Deathly Wedding Woes

Deadly Secrets

A Maddie Brook Mystery

Innvitation to Murder

Circle-D Saga Trilogy

Endless Circle

Moment in Time

Gun for Hire

Novels:

Frontier Heart

Reflections: A Sentimental Journey

Short Story:

Courtship of Laura

Acknowledgments

A special thank you to Anna Aysen of Fiverr for her excellent beta reading service, her thoroughness, her encouragement, and her dedication to providing a detailed manuscript review.

A Meadowood Mystery

Dead Secret

Nancy M. Wade

Contents

Chapter 1   1
Committee

Chapter 2   7
Debate

Chapter 3   16
Fighting Words

Chapter 4   21
Bicentennial

Chapter 5   25
Scandal

Chapter 6   32
Candidate Support

Chapter 7   38
Anniversary

Chapter 8   43
Mob Rule

Chapter 9   47
Literary Sleuthing

Chapter 10   53
Societas Liberorum Hominum

Chapter 11   58
Confession

Chapter 12   64
Call to Action

Chapter 13   69
Society Snoop

Chapter 14   76
R.I.P.

Chapter 15   85
Adele

Chapter 16   94
Woodland Design

Chapter 17   99
Puzzle Pieces

Chapter 18   104
Three Strikes You're Out

Chapter 19   111
Wyatt

Chapter 20   117
Exposed

Chapter 21   122
Revenge

Chapter 22   127
Election

Author Biography   133
Excerpt: Reunion with Death   135
Excerpt: Deathly Wedding Woes   137
Excerpt: Berry Little Murder   139

Chapter One

Committee

Sneaking a look at the clock, I tapped my foot as I watched our last customer finish her tea and scones, then browse among the delicate tea cup sets and crocheted cozies before coming to the counter to check out. I was getting antsy.

"Thank you for coming. I hope you enjoyed yourself. I know you'll love using that adorable cozy at home; it's perfect for keeping your teapot warm," I said with a smile and handed the woman her bagged cozy and receipt as I hastened her to the door.

"I can't wait to show it to my friend Miriam. We'll be back," she enthused as she exited the tea shop. The bell over the door jingled as she left.

A glance at the clock on the wall confirmed it—two o'clock, closing time. Finally. It had been a hectic morning.

"Set the lock and flip the closed sign before anyone else pops in," said Anna. She cleared the small table. Juggling cups and plates in one hand, she headed to the kitchen.

I did as Anna suggested, then finished clearing the remaining tables and wiped them all clean. With a quick look around our quaint tea shop, I assured myself we were ready for the campaign committee meeting starting in the next half-hour.

There were days when I almost pinched myself, not believing this wonderful place was really mine, at least fifty percent of it. My dream had come true the day Anna Thompson had agreed to go into business with me and we purchased the shop. Anna and I had been instant friends from the time she and her husband Chuck moved into the area from Texas about six years ago. Anna's quirky sense of humor and homespun common sense conquered most situations. The fact that she had a son Stevie, born during her change of life, kept her young. Plus it gave us something in common since our sons were the same age, despite Anna being close to twenty years my senior. Anna was a tireless worker; I only prayed I had her stamina when I got to be her age.

We named our venture the A&M Tea Shop. For the past year, we had devoted all our energy to growing and marketing our enterprise, and now the quaint tea shop was a popular tourist attraction in Meadowood.

Our Victorian English tea shop contained small bistro tables with white linen tablecloths, adorned with tiny bud vases; they sat two or three guests comfortably. We served a variety of flavorful teas using delicate porcelain tea sets and miniature tea pots. The local bakery, Martha's Delites, was owned by a dear friend, Martha Parker, and provided delicious scones for our customers. We supplemented our baked offerings with muffins and cookies that Anna and I baked in the shop's kitchen. The addition of various petite tea sandwiches completed our daily menu. The atmosphere of the shop was restful and rather feminine with its graceful chintz upholstery and curtains. Decorative floral grapevine wreaths hung on the walls. Display cases filled with knit tea cozies, delicate demitasse teacups, and a collection of sugar bowls and creamers added to our customer's interest and boosted our sales.

Anna filled the tea kettles and started a fresh pot of coffee as I arranged an assortment of pastries from Martha's bakery onto a two-tiered tray. I placed several coffee mugs on the counter, ready for our expected guests.

"Everyone should arrive soon," Anna commented as she poured cold milk into a creamer and set it next to the sugar bowl.

"We're ready. I'll go check the door."

Leaving the kitchen, I walked to the front entrance and took up my watch post. I spotted Colleen and Aunt Fran coming down the walk. Two of my friends and cub scout mothers, Barb Williams and Carol Goodwin, hurried after them as they all approached the shop. Unlocking the door, I ushered everyone inside then closed up again.

"Hey everyone. Take a seat wherever you like. Who wants coffee and who prefers tea? As it happens, we have both on hand," I joked.

"Tea for me," Colleen and Barb both ordered.

"I need a strong cup of coffee," remarked Aunt Fran.

"Me too," said Carol.

"Okay, coming right up," I said as I dashed to the kitchen.

Anna and I carried the tray of drinks and pastries from the kitchen. After serving everyone, we joined them for a well-deserved break before starting the meeting.

"Who's watching the store?" I asked my Aunt Fran as I munched on a cherry Danish then sipped my tea. "Ah, that's so good."

"Mmm, Betty as usual. I'm so lucky to have her; she practically runs the place some days. Especially now with the campaign keeping me so busy." Fran took a swallow of the hot coffee.

"Okay. Shall we get down to it?" Colleen asked as she pulled a notebook and pen from her purse.

Colleen Callahan Wythe flicked her shoulder-length auburn hair behind her ears and looked expectantly at us. Colleen, with her Irish emerald-green eyes and sprinkle of freckles across her nose, looked so pretty and fragile that most people made the mistake of not taking her seriously. Being friends since children and throughout our college years, I knew better to never underestimate my friend. I'm sure the teachers and students at the Meadowood Elementary School, where Colleen presided as principal, also knew her soft-spoken commands were meant to be followed. Now she took control of my aunt's mayoral campaign in her organized and methodical manner.

"Tonight's debate will be critical. Fran must explain her vision for the town and provide a sharp contrast to Donald Dickson's past record and her future plans for Meadowood. You're both small business owners ... you with the dress shop and Dickson runs the pharmacy. You're both members of the Chamber of Commerce but that's as far as the similarities go. We need to show voters the important differences that are key to our town's future."

I clapped my hands and grinned at my friend. "Maybe you should make the campaign speeches!"

"She's right. People need to learn the difference between Fran and Dickson. The man is up to something. I have it on good authority that scalawag's scheming to bring in some mining company to our region. That worries me," said Anna in her western twang as she sat back in her chair and crossed her arms. At times like this, when riled up, Anna's Texan roots and western drawl became more obvious.

"What good authority? I've heard rumors too but haven't been able to confirm the facts," Fran said.

"Teresa Maxwell at Cut and Curl told me she heard about Dickson's idea to allow fracking outside of town from Polly Ames. Polly works as a part-time housekeeper for Adele Dickson. Polly over heard it first hand when she was dusting in the parlor and the mayor was talking on the phone. Naturally she told Teresa." Anna nodded her head as if that proved the information was legitimate. After all, everyone knew that the hairdresser held the rank of biggest gossip in town. If you wanted to know the latest news, you asked Teresa.

Barb and Carol both laughed at Anna describing the circuitous route of gossip but agreed it was likely gospel.

"If Polly heard Dickson talk about fracking on the phone, he must be confident that he's got the deal in the bag. What does he have to gain by a mining company drilling for coal or gas? Sounds like a potential payoff or cut of the profits. I'll try to learn more," I said as we all nodded in agreement about Dickson's shady plan.

"What do you need us to do, Colleen? Carol and I can put up posters or make phone calls. Just say the word," Barb offered.

"I need you gals to plaster the town in posters. Let's see Andrews for Mayor announcements right next to the bicentennial banners on every store front. On parade day, hand out campaign buttons to every spectator. When it gets closer to election day, we'll all make phone calls to remind people to get out and vote for Fran Andrews," Colleen said.

Finishing my cup of tea, I glanced at my aunt. She'd make a great mayor. I felt so proud of her.

Frances Andrews, my mother's sister, was an attractive widow who owned and operated the best dress shop in Meadowood called Frannie's Frocks. Fran had left her California home and returned to Meadowood following her husband's death, some thirty years ago. She worked on annual food drives and whatever committees in town needed her energy. Plus, she generously invested in the A&M Tea Shop to help her favorite niece. I loved my aunt dearly; at times, I felt closer to her than my mother and not just because we favored each other with our dark blonde hair and blue eyes. The only difference in our appearance was the handful of gray strands in her hair and the extra pounds curving my hips and thighs. My aunt was almost twenty years my senior, but slimmer and more physically active than me. She was a force to be reckoned with and hard to match.

I rose to carry my tea cup into the kitchen. Eyeing my circle of friends, I asked, "Anyone want a refill?"

Judging by the shake of heads, I gathered up the other empty cups and headed for the kitchen. Fran followed me.

"Hey, I just wanted to ask you ... you're okay with me using Colleen as my campaign manager, right? You know I love you dearly and think you'd do a great job, but honestly you've got so much on your plate now, I didn't want to burden you. I know you've been helping on the parade preparations and the bicentennial committee plus busy with your cub scout den. What with splitting your time between the tea shop, scouts, committees, and a full home life with two young boys and husband—well, I don't know how you manage as it is." Fran laid a hand on my arm and searched my eyes for understanding.

"Don't worry. Colleen is ideal as your manager; she's got the summer off from school and there's no one more organized and dedicated. You made the right choice. I'll do everything that I can to assist her. I don't feel slighted in the least."

"Thank you, Merry. I was concerned you might think I didn't consider you capable, far from it. If anyone in Meadowood knows how to get things done, it's you; well maybe right behind me, of course! Must be a family trait," laughed Aunt Fran.

We hugged each other, then returned to the tea room to hear Colleen repeat the debate starting time.

"We should be at the Oak Meadow Inn before seven o'clock."

"Sounds like a plan. See you all there," said Fran.

Chapter Two

Debate

"It will mean a lot to your aunt if the entire family is there in a show of solidarity. Naturally, I know you guys will be on your best behavior. Right? You can either sit with me or your grandparents. We've got to be there early but it's okay if you grab some Cokes and watch TV in the Buckeye Room while you wait. I realize this stuff can be boring." I studied the faces of my two sons, expecting an argument, or at the very least, some grumbling.

"It's cool. Billy and I'll find something to do until debate time. Aunt Fran is going to kick some butt!" Johnny stated. He scraped the remains from his dinner plate into the trash can before stacking the dirty dish in the sink.

"Thanks."

Watching him walk away, I had to keep reminding myself that he was a teenager now and Billy wasn't too far behind him. Where did the years go? My sons had grown into responsible young men; well, perhaps not all the time and definitely not Billy. He could still be a little scamp. I smiled as memories skidded across my mind—Billy dressed as a Martian for Halloween and covered in black dust from crawling up a coal chute in the school basement. Johnny, wiping tears from his face as he held my hand while I lay injured in the hospital. Or the time Johnny and Billy first went off to summer camp, causing me to cry ... and now high school this fall. Oh my, suddenly I felt terribly old!

Shaking off my nostalgia, I focused on the task ahead and the upcoming debate. After our afternoon meeting, I did a quick internet research on the mining industry in our state and the shocking details of fracking. I printed out a page of key facts for my aunt to use during her debate points. The threat to the environment loomed as a major point she could argue, let alone the disruption to our community and economy. Johnny was right ... Fran is going to kick butt when she divulges Dickson's secret plans.

"Mroww," Mittens reminded me he needed his dinner too. His warm furry presence wound his way around my legs.

I stooped to give the orange and white tabby cat a knuckle rub on his head. Mittens arched his back and flicked his tail as he padded over toward his empty bowl, then turned and stared at me with his topaz colored eyes. My furry baby's patience only lasted so long before he pointedly meowed again.

"You're not starving, you know. However, since you've been a good boy and have left those birds alone for once, I'll treat you to some tuna."

My cat loved to startle the cardinals and robins who visited the bird feeder hanging from the deck railing. Mittens stalked the birds, which screeched and took flight with a flap of their wings. He never caught them and sometimes I think he only menaced them for fun or to claim his turf.

Mittens had become an integral part of our family ever since we'd brought him home at six weeks old. Over the past ten years, I could always count on him to sit and listen to me when others never had the time. He was a comfort and loving pet who seemed to sense when I felt troubled.

I spooned the tuna into his dish and placed a fresh bowl of water next to it. With a stroke of his silky back, I scratched his ears and gave him one last warning. "Stay out of trouble while I'm gone."

Grabbing my purse, notebook, and car keys, I headed toward the door. "C'mon guys! Let's go. I don't want to be late."

Johnny and Billy bounced down the stairs; Billy jumping off the last two steps. I waggled my finger at him in silent admonition.

"Is Dad coming?" asked Billy as we left the house.

"He's on duty tonight. We'll probably see him there with Tony."

Unlocking our new white SUV with a beep of the key fob, we all climbed into the car. My Santa Fe still contained that new car smell; a vast difference from the ten-year-old maroon minivan I used to drive. The poor thing had provided years of service hauling cub scouts plus family and logged over a hundred and fifty thousand miles, but it had developed too many mechanical problems to be reliable and too costly to repair. It was time to retire it to that huge heaven for old cars, otherwise known as the junkyard. Luckily, the income I earned at the tea shop made a new car possible ... something that would never have happened with only my past Avon sales.

Turning the corner from our street onto Park Avenue, the sight of so many banners and flags flying from every lamp post amazed me. Meadowood was gearing up for its bicentennial celebration and parade. Everyone in town was excited and tried to outdo each other with decorations. The town spirit and pride was a palpable thing you could feel in the air.

We left downtown and continued on the road toward the debate location being hosted by the League of Women Voters and Blake Garrett at his inn. Oak Meadow Inn sprawled over forty-five acres of ground within a short drive just outside Meadowood's city limits.

I parked the car in the side lot. The boys and I walked toward the front entrance of the inn. Every time I came here, the beauty of the place struck me. The exterior boasted rough granite stone walls with a charcoal slate tiled roof, floor to ceiling windows, and two wide brick patios that overlooked terraces graced with lush gardens and artfully shaped topiary trees. A lovely gazebo located off the rear terrace provided a romantic setting for wedding ceremonies. Taking a deep breath, I inhaled the delicate rose and honeysuckle scents from the garden.

Guests staying at the inn dined in the Kenyon, a four-star rated gourmet restaurant on the premises, or the fun Buckeye Room sports lounge. Activities included playing the lush, nine-hole golf course or leisurely fishing in the nearby trout-filled stream. Many guests simply relaxed at the spa and luxurious pool on site and enjoyed a drink at the patio bar. The hotel claimed the privilege of hosting two United States Presidents and four senators during the years since its construction in 1948.

Entering the lobby, a person's eye was drawn to the bold timbers stretched across high cathedral ceilings in the great room. Bright patterned area rugs softened the hardwood floors and reflected the jewel-toned fabrics of the sofas and chairs grouped near the tall stone fireplace. Framed landscape paintings of the region hung on cream-colored walls in the room.

We headed down the wide hallway toward the banquet room. The path was a familiar one as I entered the hall. The last time I had been here was a year ago to discuss Colleen and Ron's wedding reception on the premises and previously when I had attended our class reunion here. Now the room contained a small stage and two podiums facing rows of seating arranged for spectators on the floor. A patriotic bunting graced the front of the stage platform.

An ear piercing squeal split the air as the sound technician adjusted the microphones and speakers on the stage. My hands instantly flew to cover my ears until it ended. Glancing around, I spotted Colleen and Aunt Fran standing near the patio doors.

"You guys can look around if you want. Go outside and watch the golfers or wander down to the Buckeye Room and catch a game on TV. Just stay in the area. Okay?"

"Sure Mom. No problem. Me and Billy will come back in when it's time to start. I wanna hear what Aunt Fran has to say."

"Okay." I slipped a twenty-dollar bill into his hand, then let him go.

"C'mon, Billy, let's check the place out."

As the boys headed back down the hallway, I walked toward the patio entrance and met the candidate of the hour.

"There she is," Aunt Fran said with a smile as I approached.

"How are you feeling? Any butterflies?" I asked.

"No, I'm fine. Let's go outside and sit down while the technicians finish setting up the stage. I imagine Dickson will show up soon, although I haven't seen him yet."

We found a table under the shade of an umbrella and took our seats. A waitress acknowledged us with a nod of her head as she finished taking an order at the nearby table.

"What can I bring you ladies?" she asked.

"How about three glasses of iced tea?" Aunt Fran ordered for us.

"Sure thing. Um, Mrs. Andrews, I just wanted to tell you that you've got my vote. Time for the women in this town to have a voice." She tapped her pencil on the order pad and nodded her head then spun on her heel.

"Well, that's one vote," Colleen said with a chuckle.

I opened my notebook and withdrew the printouts with the data on fracking and the companies proposing that type of mining. Handing the sheets to my aunt, I pointed at the key facts underlined with yellow highlighter.

"Hit Dickson with those numbers and see what he says. I have to admit, the reports shocked me. Look at the long range effects to our environment," I stated as my aunt perused the information.

"Good work, Merry. Based upon this report, the situation is worse than I thought.

Colleen opened her own notebook. She and Fran put their heads together to speak quietly as they reviewed key points that Fran would include in her speech.

I sipped my tea as I looked through the panoramic windows into the banquet hall. People were filing in and taking seats. The place would be filling up soon.

Rumors had been flying around town and nasty comments had been heard attributed to Donald Dickson about the widow Fran Andrews. Through it all, my aunt remained calm. I ground my teeth as I recalled the last comment I'd heard from a customer in the tea shop. The gal wasn't a local but had accompanied an older woman who was. They had whispered loudly, intending for their snide gossip to be overheard by anyone seated nearby.

"... and I heard she had an affair with a dangerous felon. He left town in the dead of night." Her head bobbed smugly.

"No! Really?" The woman had leaned closer to gain her friend's ear as they both nodded emphatically.

Seeing and hearing those two vipers, it was all I could do to not pour hot water onto their heads. I hustled them out of our shop as quickly as I could that day. Politics is dirty business. It goes without saying. But who would think that a small-town mayor's race could become so vicious? Donald Dickson, obviously behind the rumors, lost all respect in my book after that incident.

I smiled fondly at my aunt. She reached across the table and squeezed my hand. I loved her so much; I'd do anything for her and the feeling was mutual.

"Almost time," Colleen said as she checked her watch. "Let's go back inside and inspect the podium and make sure you're comfortable with the height of the microphone."

We paid our check and got up to leave. The waitress gave my aunt a wink. "Knock 'em dead," she said.

"Thank you for your support," Fran said as we left the patio.

Sitting in the front row, I saved four empty chairs for my parents and sons. Hoping they'd arrive soon to save me the awkwardness of telling more people the seats were taken, I kept scanning the room for their arrival. Finally, I spotted my mom and dad, William and Margaret Johnson, enter the hall. I stood up and waved to catch their attention. They made their way down the aisle toward me.

"Goodness! I didn't expect this kind of turnout. Did you?" my mother asked as she took the chair to my left.

"Where are the boys?" inquired my dad.

"They'll be here soon. They're in the building; probably in the sports bar eating chicken wings. I told them to hang out and enjoy themselves until debate time. Johnny was looking forward to hearing Fran though, so he'll get here on time."

I stood in front of my chair and scanned the room once again. Smiling, I waved to Barb and Ted Williams as they found chairs next to the Goodwins. I noticed Martha Parker and her family a few rows back. Most of Meadowood's population filed into the room and quickly filled the audience.

It was a big turnout, better than we had hoped for. Colleen and Fran waited near the steps leading to the stage. From my vantage point in the front row, Aunt Fran appeared to be reading over her notes while Colleen pointed to some highlighted lines.

Billy and Johnny entered the banquet room and pushed their way through the crowd. I jumped up so they could see me and waved my hand. At only five feet four inches tall, I didn't exactly tower over the surrounding crowd.

"Hey Grandmom," Billy greeted as he wrapped his arms around my mother and kissed her cheek.

She hugged him back then twitched her nose. "What is that odor? Billy you smell like an old goat." She laughed then held him at arm's length.

"What did you get into? Johnny, what were you guys doing while you waited?" I asked.

Johnny and Billy exchanged a look, then both broke out in giggles. Johnny took the seat next to me while Billy slid into the chair beside his grandfather.

"We bought some Cokes and chicken wings at that Buckeye room and watched a replay of last year's football game against Michigan. By half time, we kind of got bored so we walked around the resort. Did you know this place has a bait shop and they rent fishing poles and stuff? Really cool."

"Mm-hmm, what does that have to do with Billy stinking?" I asked.

"I didn't mean to, mom. I was only looking at the worms in the tank but some of them kind of got away and crawled up my arm," Billy tried to explain.

My father gulped a chuckle. My mother looked horrified, and I swallowed to hold back my own laughter. "Pray tell me how a worm crawled up your arm? Could it be you had your hand and arm inside that tank?"

"Sort of. I only wanted to feel the dirt; it was squishy and real dark," Billy justified his curiosity.

"Hmm, probably peat moss kept damp for worms to inhabit," my dad theorized. "I imagine peat moss carries an earthy smell." He laughed outright, not able to hide his humor any longer. "C'mon Billy, let's get you washed up before the debate begins."

The pair left by the side door and headed toward the restroom. I shook my head and sighed as I watched them leave.

"Never a dull moment," I commented. When I turned back toward the stage, I spied my husband walking toward me.

Doug looked so handsome in his new sheriff's uniform. His deputy, Tony Dalton, accompanied him.

"Hey everyone. Where's Billy?" Doug asked.

"My dad just took him to the men's room to scrub him up. Your son explored the earth worm tank in the bait shop."

"Say no more; I can well imagine that stink," Doug said.

"So are you guys here to keep peace in case the debate gets exciting?" I asked with a grin and nod toward our current mayor approaching the stage location.

"Let's just say we're here to make sure everyone behaves."

Tony Dalton stood off to one side with his hat in hand. I caught his eye and smiled at him, causing him to blush.

"Hello Sergeant. Congratulations on your promotion."

"Um, ah, thank you Missus Gardner," Tony stammered.

"See you later," Doug said as he pressed a quick kiss on my cheek.

I watched him approach Mayor Dickson. The mayor held out his hand to Doug, who took it in a strange handshake with three fingers overlapped. How odd. I never saw Doug do that before. It reminded me of something, but I couldn't put my finger on it.

Chapter Three

Fighting Words

"Ladies and gentlemen, will everyone take a seat? The League of Women Voters welcome our two mayoral candidates and citizens to a special debate. Let's hear a warm round of applause for Mayor Donald Dickson of the Republican party and the opposing Democratic candidate, Frances Andrews," Blake Garrett announced.

Donald Dickson and Fran Andrews both climbed the short steps onto the stage and moved to their respective podiums. The audience applauded both candidates as they smiled broadly and waved to the crowd.

Blake Garrett held a microphone in hand then moved toward the center of the stage between the candidates.

"Tonight's moderator is someone you all know. A woman who's a pillar of our community, the president of the Meadowood School Board, and the director of the League of Women Voters ... please welcome Georgia Simmons."

Garrett turned the microphone over to Georgia. Another round of polite clapping before Georgia raised her hand and motioned everyone to silence.

"We'll start with a two minute opening statement from each candidate then we'll begin a sequence of questions. A flip of a coin earlier awarded Mayor Dickson first round," Georgia stated. She stepped off the stage and took a seat facing the contestants; she held a stop watch in her hand.

I studied Donald Dickson's face as he addressed the audience. Stern lines on his brow and around his mouth caused him to look severe, almost angry. He directed his remarks to the audience in a solemn voice normally reserved for a eulogy.

"My fellow citizens ... in my next term of office I pledge the growth of business and industry for our town and the increase of wealth for its citizens. Meadowood must look toward the future for sustained growth," Dickson stated.

He droned on for another minute, but I scarcely listened as I focused my attention on the people sitting near me and tried to judge their reaction. I glanced at my aunt as she kept a smile on her face and prepared to make her opening statement.

The mayor took a seat and nodded toward Fran when she approached the podium. She inclined her head to him, acknowledged the moderator, then faced the audience.

"Good evening, everyone. Thank you for coming out tonight. Most of you know me, but for those who do not, my name is Frances Andrews and I've lived in Meadowood close to thirty years now. I own Frannie's Frocks, a small dress shop in town. I believe Meadowood is the best representation of the living history and people of this region. It's a town with integrity and respect for that history. My administration would promote that history with emphasis on tourism and the addition of a museum devoted to the town's past. I believe in increasing revenue for business and townsfolk while preserving the richness of our community. Not jeopardizing it, like my opponent, by encouraging industry and mining that would rape our environment," Fran declared. The crowd murmured, and some gasped at her language.

I clapped my hands loudly, prompting others to follow suit until the room echoed with the sound. Georgia Simmons rose from her seat and ascended the stage to face the audience.

"Thank you candidates. We will now allow a round of questions from the audience. Each candidate will answer and offer a rebuttal as needed. The first question comes from journalist Trixie Jones of the Knox County Tribune. Miss Jones, please stand and state your question."

"Thank you. This question is for Mayor Dickson. Mister Mayor is it true that you've been in negotiation with the Ferguson Corporation that promotes natural gas mining in the county?" asked Trixie Jones.

"No. That's a false allegation," Dickson said bluntly, with no further explanation.

Trixie Jones faced Aunt Fran as she addressed her next question. "Mrs. Andrews is it true you were involved in a personal relationship with a known felon here in Meadowood about three years ago? Can you elaborate on the nature of that relationship?"

My anger simmered at the audacity of the reporter's question. It repeated the vile rumor gossiped by those two old biddies in my shop. I waited to hear how my aunt would handle the slander.

"First of all, my personal life is just that—personal. The gentleman you refer to was my friend. He was not a felon. He operated a small butcher shop in Meadowood until forced to move away. I am at liberty to say that Samuel Tilley was under the protection of the federal witness protection agency. That's all I'll say on the matter," Fran spoke firmly in an even tone, not showing any animosity toward the reporter. I certainly couldn't have answered her that coolly.

Georgia Simmons took the microphone again and flicked her hand, indicating that the reporter was finished.

"We'll take the next question from Meredith Gardner," she said, acknowledging my hand in the air.

"I'd like this question answered by both candidates. Could you explain what the term *fracking* means and what would be the effect on

Meadowood if we allowed that process?" I said with a controlled smile and stood with my chin up and met the mayor's gaze unflinchingly.

The mayor cleared his throat and faced the crowd then glared at me as I stood before him. "Fracking is an abbreviated phrase for hydraulic fracturing. It's a process of creating fractures in rocks by injecting fluid into the cracks to widen them. It's used in mining."

Fran nodded to me then directed her response to the man next to her. Dickson stood with clenched fists and a scowl on his face.

"Mayor Dickson is correct in his definition of fracking; however, he neglected to explain that this high pressure drilling produces millions of gallons of wastewater. Polluted wastewater runs off into our streams, lakes, and ground water. It's also absorbed into the earth and causes a detrimental impact on the wild life and fauna in the area. Studies have not yet concluded what it's danger may be to humans. Fracking will also lower the value of residential land and homes because of the increased truck traffic, and additional power lines required, not to mention the noise."

A low grumble vibrated in the room. Blake Garrett raised his hand demanding to be recognized. I sat back down and allowed him to speak.

"Mayor Dickson, is this true? I think the public has the right to know if our properties are at risk. As manager of the Oak Meadow Inn and Resort, I'm responsible for both the physical property and the value of the investment held by multiple stockholders. Are you planning on promoting a mining operation outside Meadowood?" Garrett demanded.

"There are no contracts with Ferguson mining. I ordered a preliminary study performed; I'll admit to that, but it was with the purpose of bringing revenue into the community," Dickson said as he defended his position.

My aunt stepped forward to comment as further mumbles filled the room.

"Mayor Dickson, if I find out otherwise, you'll have to deal with me. That's not a threat, it's a promise. Folks, if I am elected your mayor, I promise you that no fracking or mining will be outside our city limits or within the surrounding countryside. Fracking ruins the land and even falls outside numerous federal environmental regulations such as the Clean Air Act and the Clean Water Act. That kind of revenue is not worth the negative impact on our town and people," Fran concluded.

Johnny and Billy jumped up and whistled shrilly while a resounding applause rang throughout the room. I grinned from ear to ear in my admiration for my aunt.

I noticed Mayor Dickson's red face as he blustered and huffed. He stepped off the stage and stormed out the side door. His action signaled the end of the discussion. Friends and family gathered around Fran in a tight circle to congratulate her on the successful debate.

Chapter Four

Bicentennial

Horns honked. Trumpets blared and drums pounded by the high school band. Voices shouted over the cacophony of sound as committee members struggled to organize the chaos of the parade lineup. I had my own problems as leader, trying to assemble my bunch of rambunctious cub scouts.

In the town square, colorful banners and flags fluttered in the breeze, celebrating the bicentennial founding of Meadowood. The historic brick and clapboard buildings with their gables and dormers contained Meadowood's thriving businesses and store fronts along the central thoroughfare into town. Banners and buntings adorned every business, competing to showcase the city's rich history and to commemorate its 1824 birth—proof the entire city celebrated its bicentennial.

Finally, vehicles lined up behind the grand marshal to begin the parade toward the waiting citizens and spectators of Meadowood. I waved to Aunt Fran as she climbed into Colleen's sporty convertible and perched on top of the rear seat, ready to engage the crowd. The procession moved forward.

Our scout troop, dressed in crisp uniforms that proudly displayed numerous achievement badges, marched after the creeping cars. My son

Billy kept nervously looking back over his shoulder at me or his assistant leader, Ted Williams on his right, as we marched. The boys tried to maintain a straight line and even pace. Adjusting the yellow scout leader kerchief around the collar of my blue uniform blouse, I did a little skip to get back in step with the troop as we proceeded down Park Avenue.

The high school band strutted in a formation of neat rows behind us as they played lively patriotic tunes. The sound of drums and brass instruments reverberated in the air as the parade wound its way through town. Bright red firetrucks slowly followed everyone as they progressed down the center street, honking their loud fog horns with firemen waving to the crowds. Between the band, fire truck horns, and crowds cheering, the noise level was deafening. I hardly caught my name being yelled and turned to spot my parents among the excited spectators happily cheering us on. Smiling, I returned their exuberant wave.

Dignitaries had followed the grand marshal, riding in open convertible cars. Mayor Dickson sat in the back seat of a sleek vintage red Cadillac. Seeing him alone, I wondered where his wife Adele was. He gestured to his supporters, reminding them to vote and re-elect him. Retired Sheriff Edgar Simmons and his wife Georgia rode in a restored Model-T Ford. Members of the Chamber of Commerce smiled and waved to citizens as they passed. The chamber businessmen perched on a decked-out float symbolizing the prosperity of their fair community. Volunteers built the float on the back of a flat-bed truck loaned by a local farmer. Kids from the 4H Club had labored for a month to create all the float decorations representing the agricultural bounty in our county and the attractions of our rural community.

Colleen's bright yellow Mustang followed the float flatbed with Aunt Fran waving to her campaign supporters. Two bright banners draped across the hood and trunk of the car proclaimed her candidacy for mayor of Meadowood.

I spotted my husband standing in front of the bank, watching the parade progress and keeping an eagle eye on the proceedings. Sheriff

Douglas Gardner—he took his recent promotion very seriously and vowed to protect his community and citizens.

Baskets of vibrant red, white, and blue petunias hung from every lamppost along the central route, adding a splash of color to the scene. It appeared the entire population of Meadowood was present. Spectators, young and old, lined the sidewalks, cheering on the parade participants and waving flags. The atmosphere was festive as the town came together to celebrate its past and looked forward to a bright future.

The parade culminated at the wide park grounds adjacent to the Meadowood Elementary School. The flat-bed float pulled into the parking lot and dignitary cars parked alongside it or behind. Band members, scout troops, and townsfolk all dispersed to run toward the line of food trucks and vendors waiting to serve the hungry crowd in the park.

Delicious smells tempted palates as hot dogs, burgers, and French fries sizzled, along with buttery roasted corn-on-the cob served on wooden skewers. Funnel cakes dusted in cinnamon sugar, flavorful snow cones, or mouth-watering candy apple taffy provided sweet treats. Vendors poured cups of thirst-quenching iced tea and gallons of tart lemonade. The smells and tastes rivaled the best summer fair. My mouth salivated, debating on which delectable food I'd treat myself to after that long walk. I followed the crowd that had swallowed my sons, Billy and Johnny. Luckily, I had provided both boys with enough money ahead of time to buy their own food after the parade. I wasn't concerned they'd go hungry. Growing boys were eating machines. Also, I didn't worry they'd get lost or get into trouble in a small town where everybody knew everybody else. One of the benefits and detriments of small town living.

"The boys behaved really well. I was pleased, weren't you?" asked Ted Williams as he stood in line for a funnel cake.

I nodded to my assistant scout leader. "Yes, they did a great job. All those hours you practiced marching sure paid off."

A woman's scream suddenly rent the air and pierced through the layers of noise and voices filling the park. Georgia Simmons stood next to the red convertible and pointed in horror at the mayor's prone body.

I broke away from the waiting food line and ran toward the commotion. My head pivoted left and right as I scanned the crowd, looking for my husband or any sheriff's deputies to reach the scene.

I arrived next to the car at the same time Doug did. He and I exchanged a look in silent communication. Sirens sounded, and people cleared a path as the emergency vehicles neared. We knew they were too late ... the mayor was dead.

Amidst this gay scene and harmonious celebration, Mayor Dickson lay slumped over in his seat. A tiny round hole in his chest dribbled blood onto his otherwise pristine white shirt. Droplets of water beaded on top of the Cadillac's smooth leather seat. A scrap of ribbon and a campaign button lay at his feet.

"Looks like he was stabbed directly into the heart."

"Who would commit such a horrible deed on a day meant for joy and unity?" I wondered aloud.

Doug shook his head as he assumed control of the scene.

Little did I know, this shocking act was just the beginning of unraveling one of Meadowood's well-kept secrets.

Chapter Five

Scandal

Headlines screamed murder as I read the morning issue of the Knox County Tribune. I continued skimming the newspaper as I laid it on the kitchen counter and reached for the pot of hot coffee to begin my morning. The same reporter present at the debate described the mayor's murder in lurid detail then recapped the previous evening's political discussion. Jones dared to imply that the mayor's political opponent, Frances Andrews, had threatened him during the debate. She even went so far as describing Fran as a mobster's past mistress.

The very idea of my aunt hurting anyone, let alone killing the mayor, was ludicrous. My anger boiled the more I thought about the slanderous article written by Trixie Jones. That woman was going to get a piece of my mind.

Doug entered the kitchen and reached for the coffee as I brooded over the morning news. He took one look at my face and recognized all the signs of a volcano about to erupt.

"What's wrong?"

"What's wrong is that reporter spreading lies about my aunt! Just look at this headline. She's all but accusing Aunt Fran of killing the mayor," I fumed.

Doug picked up the paper, scanned the article, then tossed it back onto the counter. He drank his coffee while finishing the plate of scrambled eggs I had cooked for him. Grabbing a muffin, he started toward the door.

"Don't you have anything to say about this pack of lies?"

He shrugged his shoulders. "Gotta go, babe. I don't know when I'll be home. If you need me, call my cell," he said as he strapped on his belt and revolver.

"Doug, you haven't forgotten our anniversary dinner tomorrow night, have you? We're supposed to celebrate with Ron and Colleen. I made reservations for us at the Kenyon and everything."

"I didn't forget, but I also didn't expect to have a murder drop into my lap either. I can't promise I'll stay the entire evening, but I'll meet you there. What time is dinner?"

"Seven. I can ride with Anna and Chuck; they're coming too. We thought we'd celebrate our shop's success along with everyone's wedding anniversaries."

"Sounds good. I'll talk to you later," he said.

I ran to him and threw my arms around him then kissed him thoroughly. "Be careful out there. I love you."

"Always."

I watched him through the window as he climbed into the police cruiser and slowly drove away.

Billy and Johnny hopped out of the SUV as soon as I pulled into Ted William's driveway. Anna arrived right behind me with her son, Stevie. The boys all carried backpacks loaded with swimsuits, towels, and an extra dry T-shirt.

"You sure you don't mind our guys tagging along?" I asked Ted.

"Hey, no problem. Barb's got the day off from work and we thought we'd spend a full day at the lake. You know Joey would rather have his friends with him than just hanging out with boring parents," Ted said with a laugh. "All right if we don't get back until after eight?"

"Of course. Here's a container of sandwiches from our shop plus a zip-lock bag of oatmeal cookies to add to your picnic feast. Do you need anything else?" I asked as I handed Ted the food-filled tote bag.

"Thanks. We're good. This is plenty."

"Well, have a good time. You guys behave and listen to Ted. I better not hear any bad reports," I warned my sons before giving them each a hug. "See you later."

Anna and I each drove to the tea shop and parked around the corner on the side street. Unlocking the back door, we left the closed sign in the front window while we did a quick inventory of stock in the kitchen pantry.

I made a list as Anna considered how many jars of mayonnaise, tuna, pickles, and other key ingredients we needed. We were short on fresh herbs and fruit as well. We'd been so busy over the past two months that we were low on just about everything.

"With the kids being at the lake all day, gives us a perfect chance to run into Columbus to the food warehouse and farmer's market to stock up on supplies," I commented.

"Mm-hmm. Add black pepper and paprika to that list. Guess that does it. Want to take my car or yours?" asked Anna.

"Let's take mine; it's in the street. You can leave yours parked in the lot. I've got tons of room in the back," I said.

Anna and I shut cupboard doors and gathered up our bundle of cloth shopping bags. I grabbed my purse and locked the backdoor behind us. As I walked around the corner of the building toward the car, I came face to face with Trixie Jones. We stared at one another before I blurted out my disgruntlement.

"You've got some nerve writing those lies about my aunt. If you don't want to be sued for libel, you better print a retraction of that nonsense."

"Prove it wasn't a lie," Trixie fired back defiantly.

"Fran stated during the debate that Sam Tilley was no felon and was in fact under federal witness protection. You called her a mob mistress. That's a lie and you know it. What kind of journalist are you if you don't check your facts? Why don't you interview her direct?" My voice raised in proportion to my level of frustration with the young reporter.

"She threatened Mayor Dickson; I've got it on tape. Tell me that is a lie. You can't. Everyone heard her. Are the police going to investigate her in Dickson's death or does she get a free pass because she's related to Sheriff Gardner?"

"Are you implying my husband is biased? He's an honest man and puts the law above all; you can be sure he'll investigate the facts and follow the evidence, wherever it takes him."

"I'll be watching to make sure he does!"

I pushed past her and climbed into my car. Clutching the steering wheel in an iron grip, I took several deep breaths to calm my fury before starting the engine.

"Don't let that gal get your goat. I read the article today too. It's crap. You and I know it and so do the citizens of Meadowood. No one suspects Fran of murder; the idea is ridiculous." Anna patted my arm reassuringly.

Little did we know.

Anna and I drove into Columbus and spent the morning making the rounds of large food distributors to fill our needs. We bought commercial sized cans and jars of the ingredients and spices that would supply our kitchen for another month. Next we stopped by the large open-air farmer's market and wandered among the stalls. We gathered fresh herbs, lemons, a bushel of peaches, onions, and two quarts of blueberries for muffins. Satisfied that we had bought everything on our list, we loaded my SUV and decided to head home.

"Let's stop off at Hank's for a slice of his apple pie. We can take the back road home," suggested Anna.

"Mmm, I can taste it now, all that cinnamon flavor. We deserve a treat after all the work we've done this week."

Heading east away from Columbus, I turned off the interstate highway onto Rt. 20 that led toward Amish country and home. It was a picturesque drive as we buzzed past acres of farmland with cows grazing in meadows. Amish black buggies parked next to massive red barns. Twenty minutes later, I spied the rusty sign still dangling from its post.

I slowed then carefully pulled into the wide gravel parking lot next to a faded red and yellow train car. The rusted metal sign hanging on a bracket above the roof proclaimed the place as Hank's Erie Caboose Diner. Gray dust swirled around us as we came to a stop and parked to the right of the eating establishment. As usual, several eighteen-wheelers parked side by side in the open lot. My daddy always said truckers knew the best places to eat. Hank's was no exception. The place appeared run down, but the food was the best, as we had learned on past occasions.

"Hasn't changed any," I said, getting out of the car and walking toward the diner.

"No, don't reckon it ever will," drawled Anna. She opened the screen door, and we stepped into the narrow restaurant.

The black and white checkered floor showed a trail of scuff marks down the center aisle. Faded red vinyl covered counter stools and bench seats in dining booths. A tired, yellowed philodendron plant hung in the window.

The same middle-aged waitress with salt and pepper gray hair, wearing a faded blue and white gingham apron, flashed us a friendly smile. She hustled past us with a dish-laden tray. "Be right with you gals," she said as she hurried toward a back table.

We waited until she dashed out of the kitchen and approached us. She paused as she studied our faces.

"Hey there, haven't seen you ladies in a coon's age."

"Howdy, Margie. How are you?" asked Anna. "Got a spot where I can rest these weary bones?"

"Sure thing honey. How about this booth right here? Now what can I bring you gals?" She pulled the pencil from behind her ear and grabbed an order pad from her apron pocket.

"Got any of that delicious apple pie left? We'll each have a slice and coffee for me," Anna ordered.

"Tall glass of iced tea for me, thanks, along with the pie," I said.

"Coming right up," Margie said. She scooted behind the counter, grabbed a full pot of coffee off the machine, stopped to pour hot refills for two men seated at the counter, then returned with a mug in one hand and a frosty glass of tea in the other. She was a ballet in motion. "Lemme go get those pies."

I leaned back in my seat and looked around the busy diner, filled primarily with truckers. One man looked familiar. Could it be ...?

Margie slid the plates of apple pie onto the table and started to turn back to the kitchen, but I grabbed her hand and stopped her.

"Margie, is that Big Jim?" I asked.

"Yep, sure is. He still comes in here like clock work whenever his run brings him through these parts."

"Um, I hate to ask, but does he still travel with Hilda?"

"See that stool next to him? Look under his hat. That's her urn, still riding along with him."

"Oh my goodness! I'm surprised Hank allows him to bring that urn inside the diner."

"Humph, you gonna be the one that tells him he can't? Funny how some men are so devoted to the one they love. Big Jim loved that little gal and he'll forever keep her by his side. Now you take your man ... he's devoted to you. I can tell. I've seen him in here from time to time with other deputies. No doubt about it."

"That's sweet of you to say. Thank you," I said in a soft voice.

"Can't say every man acts like that. Read in the paper that mayor of yours got himself murdered. No surprise, considering his alley cat ways. Probably some righteous husband or hussy did him in," Margie stated.

Anna sat stunned, her eyes wide.

My mouth fell open. I blinked while my forkful of pie hung mid-air between my plate and my mouth. Finding my voice again, I whispered, "Are you talking about Mayor Dickson? Did he have a girlfriend?"

"Saw him in here with some young chickie last week. The way she was giggling and hanging onto his arm, sure wasn't his wife." Margie turned back to the kitchen and left the two of us speechless.

"Holy cow! Who would have thought?" Anna snickered.

"Do you think his wandering eye might have gotten him killed? I've gotta tell Doug as soon as we get home. I wonder who the woman was?"

"Dunno. Maybe Margie can describe her to us."

"Let's ask her before we leave. Oh my gosh, wait until I tell Aunt Fran."

Chapter Six

Candidate Support

"Hello Betty. Is my aunt here?" I asked as I strolled into Frannie's Frocks. Betty stood at the register. I scanned the store but didn't see my aunt. When I looked back toward Betty, I noticed the tears in her red eyes.

"She's been arrested!" Betty cried in a fresh wave of tears.

"What? That can't be true. Doug wouldn't do such a thing. He knows Fran had nothing to do with Dickson's death."

"Well he and a deputy just marched her out of here less than ten minutes ago," Betty insisted as she wiped her eyes and sniffled.

"I'm going to find out what's going on. Don't worry. Why don't you close up the shop early. I'm sure my aunt won't mind."

"Thanks, but I'll stay until five o'clock like she'd expect."

I hurried out of the shop and jumped into my car. With a squeal of my tires, I peeled away from the curb and headed toward the sheriff's office.

Bursting through the outer door of the station, I stormed past the deputy on duty at the front desk and headed straight for the sheriff's inner office.

"Hey! You can't go back there," shouted the young deputy as he jumped up from his desk in hot pursuit. He skidded to a halt as he found me standing before Doug's desk, my hands on my hips and a glower on my face.

"It's okay, Billy. This is my wife," Doug said as he waved the deputy out and closed the door behind me. "I wondered how long it would take for you to get here."

"Are you out of your mind? Why did you arrest Aunt Fran?" I demanded.

"For starters, she's not under arrest. I just brought her in as a person of interest to answer some questions. You know I can't treat her any differently just because she's family."

"Where is she? Can I talk to her?"

"I'll give you five minutes with her. She's in the interview room. But Merry, stay out of this. I won't have you meddling in my case. Do you understand?"

I stood my ground and glared at my husband. "Do you understand that anyone could have killed Dickson? Even his mistress?" I gave Doug a smug smile as his face registered surprise. "Yes, that's right. I learned earlier today that he was cheating on his wife. Wonder what else Dickson was hiding."

"Are you sure? I've never heard rumors about a mistress."

"That's because our mayor kept his sweetie over in Pottstown but used to treat her to a meal at Hank's Diner. Anna and I stopped in there today on our way home from shopping in Columbus. Margie, the waitress, was very informative. Go talk to her."

"I will. But promise me you'll stay out of my investigation."

"I don't see how I can when you go around accusing innocent people. All I'll promise is to share anything I find with you, which is probably more than you'll do. Donald Dickson was up to something with mistresses and that fracking business and I'm going to find out what. Now can I speak to Aunt Fran?"

"C'mon, she's across the hall. I swear ... one of these days Merry, you're going to push me too far," Doug said through gritted teeth. He pushed open the door and ushered me into the windowless room.

I rushed to my aunt's side and wrapped my arms around her in a fierce hug. We clung to each other for a few minutes then she sat back down and I took the chair next to her.

"It's all right. Doug is just doing his job. There's nothing to worry about," Fran said in a soft-spoken voice.

Once again, I marveled at her calm demeanor. "Do you remember Margie from Hank's Erie Caboose Diner? Anna and I stopped in for pie today on our way home from shopping. She told us a fascinating story about Dickson and a sweet young thing on his arm. Seems the mayor fooled around on his wife. Now I ask you, who had a better motive for murder … the neglected wife or the jilted mistress?"

"Hmm, that's a bit of news I didn't expect. Donald really had his fingers in a few pies, didn't he? I still think we need to learn more about his business dealings."

"I think so too. That's where I'll start my search," I said.

"What search? Meredith Gardner, you aren't planning on getting involved in this investigation, are you?" Fran clasped my hands, a frown creasing her smooth skin.

"Of course I am. How can I not when my own husband arrests my dearest aunt? Just watch me."

"Trust me, the truth will come out. I'm fine. Don't jeopardize your marriage on the eve of your wedding anniversary. You're just upset and blowing off steam. Use that intelligent mind of yours and don't let your hot emotions get ahead of your better judgement. Listen to me, I'm serious. I appreciate your help but don't go running off half-cocked."

Taking a deep breath, I studied her face and conceded. She was right. My emotions were getting the better of me. I needed to think straight, but that didn't mean I wouldn't research Donald Dickson's past and current business.

I stood and gave her another hug then paused with my hand on the doorknob. "You're right. I'll calm down and think first before I act."

"Good. I'll be out of here soon. We can talk tomorrow."

The next day, it was business as usual at the A&M Tea Shop. Anna and I performed our usual ballet moving about the kitchen and dining room as we prepared food and served customers. The bell above our door jingled gaily throughout the day as people came and went. Customers raved over the fresh blueberry muffins we had baked first thing that morning. They were a big hit.

I wiped my hands on a dish towel before plating the last two muffins and poured a cup of Darjeeling tea to serve a single lady waiting at the window table. She had entered the shop, browsed the shelf of tea pots, then sat at the small, secluded table.

"Hello. Welcome to the A&M Tea Shop." I set the plate and tea cup before her.

"Thank you. These look marvelous."

"Just baked this morning with blueberries picked up from the farmer's market yesterday. Let me know if there is anything else that I can bring you," I said with a smile, and turned to go back into the kitchen.

"Um, could you perhaps sit down for a moment?"

Puzzled, I paused as I moved back to her table and slid out a chair. She had my full attention.

"I, uh, heard you're related to Frances Andrews. Is that right?"

"Yes. She's my aunt. Why do you want to know?"

"I saw all the posters around town that she's running for mayor against Donald Dickson, or at least she was until his death. Do you think the other party will put up a new candidate?"

"Gosh, I don't know. I suppose they could if there is time between now and the election. I'm sorry ... I didn't get your name," I said as I looked at the woman across from me.

"Mrs. Ellen Ferguson. I'd like to offer my support to Fran Andrews."

I sat back in my chair. Where had I heard the name Ferguson before? And just like that, I recalled the mayor's words at the debate as he spoke of his dealings with the Ferguson Corporation. My eyes widened as I realized the significance of the woman before me.

"Are you by any chance related to John Ferguson with the mining company?"

"Yes. He's my husband. I think I may have some useful information to share with Mrs. Andrews. I'm against fracking and the destruction it causes. I heard your aunt speak about the subject a few days ago."

"I'm certain my aunt would want to talk with you. Let me call her. Can you wait?"

"I'll finish this delicious snack while you phone. Perhaps we can arrange something."

I jumped up and hurried into the kitchen and pulled my cell phone from my purse. Speedily dialing my aunt's private number, I waited for her to pick up.

"Hello?" I heard her voice answer.

"Aunt Fran. Can you run down to the tea shop right now? There's a woman here you've got to meet. Hurry. I don't know how long she can stay."

"All right. I don't understand the mystery but I'll come right now."

"Okay. Hurry." I ended the call. Grabbing the tea pot to freshen Ellen Ferguson's tea, I rushed back to her table.

Two minutes later, Aunt Fran walked into the tea shop, glanced around, then spotted me and the lone woman seated at the bistro table. Fran held out her hand to the woman and smiled.

"Hello. I'm Fran Andrews. I understand you wanted to see me. What can I do for you?"

"I believe it's what I can do for you. I've got some important information to share that will benefit your campaign.

Fran slid into the empty chair across from the woman while I stood to the side. Catching a nod from my aunt, I left them alone and scooted back to the kitchen. I busied myself by preparing a cup of coffee, preferred by my aunt, and added a plate with a strawberry scone. When I served her refreshment, the two women had their heads together, speaking softly.

Ellen Ferguson rose from her chair, laid a ten-dollar bill on the table, and quietly slipped out of the shop. I stood looking after her then turned my focus back to my aunt who sat lost in thought.

"Well? What did she say?" I asked before my curiosity killed me.

"Interesting woman. Have you ever heard of Societas Liberorum Hominum?"

"Is that Latin? What's it mean?"

"It means Meadowood has a secret society," Fran said in a low voice, her brow creased as she considered the impact of the information she'd just heard.

Chapter Seven

Anniversary

After dropping the boys off at their grandparent's house, I treated myself to a long hot shower with a fragrant gel and shampoo. Slipping on a cool linen sundress in my favorite shade of blue, I buckled on a pair of strappy sandals. Fluffing my hair and tweaking a few curls around my ears, I added a pair of gold earrings. A touch of face powder on my nose and some pink lipstick. I was ready to go.

As I waited for Anna and Chuck to pick me up, I fed Mittens and turned on one lamp in the living room. The painting above the mantle caught my eye; a purchase we had made for our fifth anniversary many years ago. I loved that Kincaid scene, so serene and pleasing. A pair of my grandmother's antique brass candlesticks flanked it on the mantle.

I glanced about our home, satisfied with the cool sage green upholstered sofa and matching draperies in the living room and the pair of light tan recliners. A side chair covered in a sage and tan tweed fabric coordinated with the other pieces. Our Colonial two-story home wasn't fancy, but it was comfortable and serviceable with two young boys and one furry baby.

I had met Doug Gardner at college when he enrolled after serving in the Army. He swept me off my feet; love at first sight, and we married soon after. I had finished my associate degree but quit school when I became pregnant with our son Johnny. Doug transferred to OSU to complete his bachelor's. He and Ron Wythe were both star players on the OSU football team; staunch friends, they were still loyal Buckeyes especially every fall season.

We had a good life and a happy one, despite the arguments that flared up from time to time. I was normally to blame. Really. I admit it. My temper got the better of me on far too many occasions. It was a wonder Doug could keep his patience until I cooled off. Funny ... we didn't fight about day-to-day household things or the kids; it usually only happened when we were both investigating a case. Doug just didn't understand my need to be involved, and I usually blamed him for not appreciating the importance of my findings. This time, things would be different. He couldn't discount historical or scientific data, and that's just what I intended to find to solve Dickson's murder.

A horn beeped, breaking my reverie. Anna and Chuck had arrived to pick me up. Doug would meet us at the resort as soon as he could get away. Colleen and Ron were driving their own car. I locked the door behind me then hopped into the back seat of Chuck's sedan and we were off.

Solar lights flickered on around the perimeter of the Oak Meadow Inn drive and parking lot. The evening air carried a sweet fragrance from the garden as the lights shimmered beneath the honeysuckle and white roses. The three of us entered the lobby, looking for Colleen and Ron. We had agreed to meet out front before proceeding to the Kenyon Room. I waved as I spotted the newlyweds standing near the large stone hearth.

Tonight would be a special celebration for all. Colleen and Ron celebrated their first wedding anniversary. Doug and I commemorated our fifteenth, plus Anna and I were recognizing our first full year of success with the tea shop. I gave Colleen a quick hug as she joined Anna and me.

"I love your dress," Colleen commented.

"Thanks. You look especially pretty too. Are those earrings new?" I asked Colleen.

Her fingers touched the sparkling emeralds gracing her earlobes. A smile stretched from ear to ear. "Ron gave these to me for our anniversary. Aren't they gorgeous?"

"Love them, especially on you. Brings out the green in your eyes."

"Will Doug be here soon? Should we go back to the dining room or wait here?" Ron asked.

"Let's go back. He'll join us soon. We've got reservations but I doubt they'll hold our table too long," I said.

We left the lobby and walked the short distance toward the premier resort dining room named the Kenyon. Colorful prints of John Audubon's bird species decorated the pale gold walls of the room. White linen tablecloths covered the tables with gold brocade upholstered chairs. A brass candle holder held a lit white taper covered by a frosted glass globe in the center of the table.

"Reservations for Gardner, party of six," I told the maître d' standing at the entrance lectern.

He led us toward a round table accommodating six chairs. The waiter held out my chair for me as Chuck and Ron did the same for Anna and Colleen.

"Thank you. My husband will join us shortly."

"Very good, madam. Enjoy your meal."

"This is so nice," commented Colleen.

"Definitely putting on the ritz," drawled Anna as she studied the menu.

"Let's order a bottle of champagne to toast our special occasions," suggested Ron. He winked at Colleen.

"Sounds marvelous! Oh, here comes Doug," I said as I spied my husband enter the restaurant. He nodded at the waiter and made his way over to our table.

"Perfect timing," Ron said as the men shook hands in greeting.

"Hope you don't mind the uniform; I've got to get back to the office after dinner," he told the rest of our party. "Did you order yet?" asked Doug as he slid into his seat next to me.

"No, actually, we just got here," I said as I patted his arm.

Doug leaned toward me and whispered in my ear, "You look gorgeous. I'm hoping we can have a private moment tonight."

Lowering my eyes, I smiled warmly at him, my heart melting. "I believe you owe me some cuddle time," I whispered back to him.

"Does that mean you forgive me for questioning Fran?"

"Of course. Sorry I flew off the handle as always. I know you're only doing your job," I replied in a soft voice.

"Hey, you two, break it up. The waiter needs our orders," Anna chided us for our intimate whispering.

I blushed guiltily and immediately focused on the menu as the waiter made his rounds. Raising my eyes to Colleen, she nodded and hid a giggle behind her hand. My friend knew me all too well. Besides, as a newlywed, I'm sure she and Ron were making romantic plans of their own.

Once we placed our orders, our waiter returned with the bottle of champagne that Ron had requested. The cork popped loudly, with a display of bubbles frothing at the neck of the bottle. We clapped our hands in appreciation as the waiter filler our glasses.

"I propose a toast," Ron said as he raised his glass. "To us ... good friends, good times, love and happiness to all."

I raised my glass and clinked it to Anna's and Colleen's as we reached across the wide table. "Best friends forever," I pledged.

"Happy anniversary, honey," Colleen's velvety voice toasted Ron.

"Fifteen years ... hard to believe it flew by so fast," I said.

"Happy Anniversary, Merry," Doug said with a kiss to my cheek.

"Congratulations to everyone, all around," Chuck chimed in.

We all sipped the sparkling champagne and nibbled on the plate of cheese puff appetizers as we waited for our meals. Conversation turned to the election.

"What happens now, Colleen, with Dickson gone? Will the

opposing party put up another candidate to run against Fran?" asked Chuck.

"Hmm, dunno. The deputy mayor, Myron Willis, has assumed the duties of mayor since Dickson's death. But I don't know whether he plans to run in his place," Colleen said with a bite into her cheese puff.

"I've seen Willis around town. He's scared of his own shadow," I snickered.

"The man is a mouse. I don't see him wanting the job permanently. Can the election be held with only one candidate?" asked Anna.

"Technically, yes. Printed ballots already contain both Donald Dickson and Fran Andrews names. People can choose to vote yes for Fran or leave it blank. If she runs unopposed, she's got the seat no matter the vote count," Colleen explained.

"Wow. I don't know if I like that idea. Wouldn't it be better if the other side nominated someone? Kind of makes her look guilty, as if she had a motive for killing him to secure the mayor's office," I speculated.

"I'll admit it doesn't put her in a favorable position. This information goes no further than this table ... but we found one of Fran's campaign buttons on the Cadillac floor board," Doug spoke in a hushed tone.

I sucked in my breath and glanced around the table at the concerned expressions on everyone's face.

"Anyone could have dropped that," I argued.

"True. That's why she was only questioned as a person of interest, not a suspect. Believe it or not, dear wife, I know how to do my job."

"I never doubted it, but some people might if that information gets out."

My words turned prophetic when the next morning, a mob of angry people picketed the sheriff's office.

Chapter Eight

Mob Rule

Angry voices shouted complaints and slurs directed toward the sheriff and his deputies as a mob of people crowded the sidewalk in front of the Meadowood Sheriff's Office. As the morning grew longer, the voices grew louder until the abusive shouting took on a threatening tone. One man hurled a rock against the front window.

"Okay, that's it," Doug stated to Tony as he stood in the doorway listening to the protests. "Haul him in, his right to peaceful protesting just ended."

Doug and Tony stepped outside with their backs against the closed office door.

"Who threw that rock?" demanded Doug. He faced the crowd with his hands on his hips and a stern expression on his face. His eyes narrowed as he scanned the group of people.

The noise quieted to a low rumbling murmur as the mob faced him. One man defiantly stepped forward.

"I did. So what. Afraid of a little rock, Sheriff? What are you doing about Mayor Dickson's murder? Edgar Simmons protected the citizens of this town for years. If he was still sheriff, Dickson would be alive.

You're in office one month and look what happened." His voice rose in strength as he spoke, firing up the crowd again.

Doug raised his hands, palms facing outward, as he sought to quiet the unrest. "Folks! Listen folks! I understand your fear and worry. My deputies and I are following every lead, every clue. I promise you we'll find the person who did this."

"You ain't looking too close to home; your wife's aunt has the best motive. What do you say to that? How come Andrews ain't sittin' in jail?" sneered another man.

Doug focused on the speaker. He didn't recognize him, and he knew most folks in town. His shaggy hair, dirty clothes, and appearance made Doug doubt if he was even a citizen of Meadowood. Perhaps a trouble-maker planted in the crowd? Who put him up to it?

"What's your name, buddy?" asked Doug as he singled out the protester.

The man shook his head and stepped backwards, blending into the crowd. Doug watched him slip away. *Mm-humph, thought so. He meant to stir up trouble.*

"I'm looking for anyone who saw the mayor's car at the end of the parade. Anyone who might have been in the lot as the parade ended when the car parked or perhaps noticed who waited nearby. Think. You may have witnessed someone or an action that didn't seem important at the time but may be vital. Please come talk to me. I need to hear from you; we're all in this together. Help me."

Heads nodded, people shuffled their feet, and the crowd dispersed. A few people turned and looked back at the sheriff, standing strong and resolute.

I glanced up as Colleen rushed into the tea shop. While I finished pouring a second cup of tea for my customer, I inclined my head toward the kitchen and signaled for her to meet me there.

"Would you like another scone?" I asked the elderly woman in front of me as my thoughts jumped to Colleen's presence. The lady shook her head no. "All right, enjoy the tea then." I carried the tea pot back to the kitchen.

Colleen's face was flushed as she accepted a cup of tea from Anna and perched on a stool by the counter. As soon as I joined the pair, Colleen grabbed my hand. I could read the terror on her face.

"What is it?" I asked as I clutched the ceramic tea pot to me, my heart racing.

"There's a mob in front of the sheriff's office. I saw Doug standing in front of the doors surrounded by angry people," Colleen exhaled in a loud whisper.

I blanched as I instantly recalled our conversation of the night before. Pulling my cell phone from my apron pocket, I quickly dialed Doug's private number. I held my breath until I heard his voice answer.

"Are you okay?" I blurted as soon as he answered.

"Calm down. I'm okay. We're all fine and the crowd is gone."

"Oh! Thank goodness! What did they want?" Now that I knew he wasn't in danger, my curiosity kicked in.

"People are upset, that's all. Losing their mayor like that in the middle of a parade that was supposed to celebrate the town ... folks were voicing their fears and doubts. Seems they think Edgar did a better job as sheriff and they don't trust me yet."

"Aargh! Who do they think has been doing the job all this time? I could just spit."

Doug made a short laugh, but I could hear the hurt in his voice. Didn't those fools know that Doug was responsible for keeping the peace in Meadowood over the last two years? It was Doug investigating and solving crimes, while Edgar Simmons gladly gave up the reins of power. Edgar was an old man that should have retired years ago but hung in there to increase his pension. The man's health declined long before the poisoning episode last Christmas that landed him in a hospital for two weeks. I think that was the final straw; Edgar's brush with death scared him into retirement.

"Spilt milk, Meredith. I'll earn their trust when I solve Dickson's murder and townsfolk realize it's my work. Don't worry, now. I've got things to do."

Doug ended the call. I held my silent cell in my hand as I stared at the floor, lost in thought.

"Hey, come back to earth! Are Doug and his deputies okay?" asked Colleen.

"Yeah, he's all right. The crowd's gone. He says people are angry because he hasn't found Dickson's murderer yet. We've got to help him," I declared. I wiped my hands on a dish towel and grabbed my purse off the coat hook.

Anna and Colleen stared at me. "What do you plan to do?"

"Anna, can you close up the shop on your own? Colleen and I need to do some research," I said with a determined look on my face.

"Where we going?" asked Colleen as I pushed her out the back door.

"Library. I need your scholarly abilities to find a secret society."

"What?!"

Chapter Nine

Literary Sleuthing

"I don't understand what we're doing at the library," complained Colleen as we pulled into the library parking lot.

"Look. If we're going to help Doug solve this murder, I figure the first thing we have to do is learn everything we can about Donald Dickson. Face it ... what do we really know about the man? Who was he? What better place to learn some history than a library?" I asked my friend as I sprinted up the tall brick steps leading toward the wide double entry doors of the Meadowood Library.

"Okay, I see your point, but still ..."

"C'mon, I'll explain later."

I rushed into the library then stopped short, causing Colleen to collide into my back. Considering my objective, I approached the front check-out desk and smiled at the library clerk.

"Where would I find biographies?" I asked in a hushed voice so I wouldn't disturb the handful of patrons reading nearby.

"Second floor, rows A through E, under Dewey decimal number 921," the clerk answered.

"Thank you." I grabbed Colleen's hand and we hurried up the staircase to the second floor.

"What do you expect to find among biographies?"

"Remember a few years ago when the town council created a *Who's Who* in Meadowood? A sort of yearbook was published with all the prominent citizens of the town. I remember old man Kirkland was highlighted as one of the founding fathers and I'm pretty sure I recall seeing Dickson included among the local businessmen."

My hand glided over the book spines as I searched the shelves. Skimming over names of authors and historians, I stopped as I found a section devoted to local people of interest.

"Here it is. I was sure I remembered running across that yearbook one time when I was helping Johnny with a school project. Yep, this is what I wanted," I said as I pulled the book off the shelf and carried it over to a nearby table.

Colleen sat next to me as we turned the pages and searched for the passage on Donald Dickson. She read out loud the biography on the past mayor.

"Hmm, Donald Dickson, born August 1964 in Mount Vernon, Ohio. He graduated from Ohio University in Athens and moved to Meadowood in 1989. Says here he married Adele Hayes and purchased the Meadowood Apothecary that same year."

"For a recent college grad, it didn't take him very long to acquire a going business concern. Wonder where he got the money? So Dickson wasn't a trained pharmacist, but he owned the pharmacy. I suppose that's true of other stores like the big chain pharmacies; just seems odd in a small town," I said as I continued to read his accomplishments.

"He joined the Chamber of Commerce and first ran for town councilman in 1998 and after that, he was elected mayor in 2005 and he's served since. Definitely a long career," commented Colleen.

"Aunt Fran would know better, but I think Adele and Donald only had one daughter and she moved away when she married. I don't think she's been back since," I said.

"All right, so now we know the facts on Donald Dickson's life. *What* did we gain by that?" asked Colleen.

"It gave us a place to start. We need to learn what Adele's life is like. What does she do all day long? What was their marriage like? I wonder when Donald started cheating on her. I'm afraid these books won't have that kind of information, but I think I know who might."

"Are you thinking a trip to the beauty salon is in order?"

"Yeah, I do believe that's our next stop. Now, just one more thing to research. Have you ever heard the term Societas Liberorum Hominum?"

"That's Latin. I'm a little rusty on my Latin studies but I think it translates to society of free men. Where did you hear that name?" Colleen asked.

"Did my aunt tell you about her meeting with Ellen Ferguson?"

"She did mention that she'd met the wife of the Ferguson Mining company and that she'd offered her support to Fran."

"Well part of that support was the suggestion that we investigate the Society of Free Men in Meadowood. It's some kind of secret society and Mrs. Ferguson seemed to think it was involved with the fracking proposal and her husband."

"Hmm, I think I understand. Was Dickson a member of this fraternity? Isn't it just like the Freemasons or something?"

"That's what we need to find out. I'm thinking maybe the history of Meadowood might include some background on the society. After all, consider the name ... society of free men, sounds like something to do with men fighting for freedom or freedom from slavery. Why else would they come up with that kind of name?"

We moved among the stacks and found Ohio history books. I searched for Northwest Territory history that included the settlement of Ohio back in the late 1790s and the establishment of the state in 1803. Colleen and I both browsed through local history books searching for any reference of the society. My eyes began to glaze over.

"This feels like looking for a needle in a haystack. We've got to narrow down our search," Colleen said.

"You're right. Let's check with the reference librarian. Maybe she can help."

Shelving the history books, we left our cubicle and approached Selma Whitehead at the librarian's desk. Selma's eyeglasses perched atop her silvery white hair that bordered a pale face with caked powder and rouged cheeks. She glanced up from her desk and pasted a polite smile on her face.

"Meredith and Colleen—how can I help you ladies?"

"Hello Miss Whitehead. How are you today?" Colleen greeted the elder lady.

"I'm researching community history. Perhaps dating back to the founding of Meadowood … for the um, bicentennial. Do you have any information on the Society of Free Men?"

The librarian's eyebrows shot up and she stared at me. I tried to paste an innocent look on my face. I glanced over at Colleen to see how she was reading the woman's reaction.

"Oh dear, we don't, ah, get many requests for that information. I, um, may have something on file. Let me check."

Colleen and I waited while the librarian entered her office and pulled open a drawer in a steel four-drawer tall cabinet. I could see typical hanging files with color-coded folders in the drawer. White typed labels attached to the folders identified subject material. Miss Whitehead, if nothing else, was the epitome of an organized librarian. I spied her pull out a folder, then hesitate and slide it back inside again. She closed the drawer and returned to us.

"Sorry, I can't help you."

"Thank you for your time," Colleen replied politely.

We walked away from the reference desk; I could feel the woman's eyes on us. I moved between an aisle of tall bookcases and pulled Colleen in after me.

Colleen slapped my hand away. "What are you doing?" she whispered.

"She's hiding something. I've got to see that file. You draw her away long enough for me to have a peek."

"Are you crazy? What if she catches you? I've got a reputation to consider. School principals aren't supposed to vandalize libraries!"

"Oh come on! This isn't vandalism. I just want to read what's in that file. It's important. You can do this. It won't be any worse than the time we sneaked into the biology lab in tenth grade and opened up all those frog cages to save them from dissection. Thinking back, that was pretty funny," I said with a snort of laughter.

"Meredith Gardner, you are always getting me involved in your high jinks. This better be worth it." She sighed heavily. "What do you want me to do?"

"Go ask Whitehead for help finding a book in one of these stacks, out of sight of her office. Keep her here for a few minutes. Let's see, ask her about this author," I said as I grabbed a book from the shelf and handed it to Colleen. Reading the title, it was a botany book on meadow flowers.

Colleen memorized the title and author then we hid the book on an upper shelf. Hopefully, it will require enough search by the librarian to provide my distraction.

"Give me five minutes to get in position near her office then you go speak with her," I said as I moved off to hide near her door.

Colleen nodded, checked her watch, then slowly returned to the librarian's desk. She cleared her throat to gain the woman's attention then smiled at her.

"Miss Whitehead, I was wondering if you could help me find a book? I've searched the shelves where the catalog says it should be, but I can't seem to find it."

"Of course dear. I'd be happy to. Where's your friend?"

"Um, ladies room. She'll be back in a second. I'm really interested in reading about a particular wildflower and I see that Barry Wilkes has a book on the subject," Colleen's voice trailed off as she followed the librarian into the stacks. She waved her hand behind her back as a signal for me to take off.

I dashed into the librarian's office and eased the file cabinet drawer open. My fingers leafed through the folders until I spied the file labeled S.O.F.M., society of free men. Pulling the document from the file, I snapped a picture of it with my cell phone then searched for additional papers in the folder. A handwritten list caught my attention, so I photographed it quickly without even reading it then tucked the file back into its folder and slid the drawer closed as quietly as I could. I hurried from the office, praying no one else saw me, then plopped into a chair and picked up a magazine just as Colleen returned with a book in hand and Miss Whitehead smiling approvingly.

"There you are. Find your book?" I asked Colleen as I stood and laid the magazine on the table next to my chair.

"Yes, exactly what I wanted. Let's check out my book and go. I've got to get home before Ron." Colleen turned to the librarian again and smiled sweetly. "Thank you for your help."

"Any time, dear. That's what I'm here for."

We scooted down the stairs, stopped at the front desk to check out Colleen's horticulture book, and flew out the door.

"I feel so guilty! Why do I let you put me in these situations all the time?" Colleen cried as we pulled away from the library.

"Relax. You did nothing wrong. You might actually enjoy that book on meadow flowers," I said with a grin.

"Please tell me you found what you needed. I can't go through that again."

"I found something. Didn't take time to study it before I got out of there. Let's go over to Martha's and get something to eat and drink. Anna has closed the tea shop by now."

"You finally have a good idea."

Chapter Ten

Societas Liberorum Hominum

Martha handed me a tall glass of iced tea along with one of her famous cinnamon rolls. Both looked delicious and reminded me I hadn't eaten since breakfast earlier this morning. Our caper at the library had caused me to miss my usual afternoon snack at the tea shop; my stomach growled in acknowledgement of the oversight.

"How's the campaign coming along?" asked Martha as she served Colleen a pastry and glass of iced tea.

"We've had positive response from most people but of course Fran decided to cancel upcoming planned events after Dickson's death," Colleen replied. She sipped her drink then glanced about the bakery.

"That makes sense, I guess. Hard to campaign against an opponent who doesn't exist any more. Merry, is Doug any closer to finding the killer?" asked Martha.

"He's working on it."

Martha Parker knew all too well what it felt like to be accused of murder when last Christmas she had become the number one suspect in the poisoning of a rival business woman. It was touch and go for awhile, until Anna and I proved the deadly mulled cider was the result of another's action and Martha was released. Remembering the harrowing holiday made me shudder; I didn't want to go through that again.

"You let me know if I can do anything to help Fran's campaign. I'll keep her poster in my window," Martha said as she returned to the kitchen.

After eating a few bites of cinnamon roll to quiet my tummy, I pulled out my cell phone and scrolled through the recent photos. I opened the picture of the document and slid the phone over to Colleen to read, expanding the image as I did so.

"This was in the file? Looks like a brief history of a fraternal organization." Colleen pointed to a date in the text. "Appears to have been founded in 1810. That's after Ohio officially became a state but much earlier than our town's founding."

"That's what I thought too. From what I read in the file, this society was exclusive to white men only, no women, banded together to create their own laws and establish a community outside the ruling of the government. Looks like landowners qualified for membership, no share-croppers, or servants."

"A common occurrence in colonial days, especially among settlers in more remote territories that relied upon their own governance for survival. They would have made a pact to protect each other and offer assistance to neighbors against all intruders," Colleen remarked as she nibbled on her pastry.

"I get that, but why would something like this need to exist in today's world? Why keep it a secret? Have you ever heard of this Society of Free Men before now?"

I pulled up the next image of the handwritten note and my eyes widened as I read the list of names. Members of the society? Expanding the image, I showed it to Colleen.

"Oh my! Ron's name is on that list. Look, Doug's name has been penciled in on the bottom of the list too."

"It would seem our husbands are a member of a secret society. Now the question is, why did Ellen Ferguson think it was important for us to learn about this group and what does it have to do with Donald Dickson's murder?" I asked.

"You can be sure that I plan on asking Ron as soon as I get home. I can't believe he didn't tell me he belonged to this organization."

"Well, considering that Ron didn't even tell you he had a twin brother before your wedding, I'd say the man is an expert at keeping secrets. But I certainly intend to question Doug, that's for sure."

We both nibbled on our pastries, lost in thought after discovering our husbands' names among the list of members for a secret fraternal society we knew nothing about. I kept thinking about Doug's name being added to the bottom of the list. Edgar Simmons was also on that list. Did that mean that becoming sheriff qualified for membership? Of course. It's the only thing that made sense. I recalled the handshake that I witnessed between Doug and Donald Dickson. The mayor was included on the roster; the handshake must be a sign of recognition among members, like the Freemasons.

"I think we need to chat with Teresa when we leave here. Let's try to learn more about Adele Dickson and her marriage," I said as I sipped my iced tea and wondered what other secrets were hidden in the lives of our town's citizens.

"Okay. Sounds like a good idea to me."

Teresa Maxwell owned the beauty shop Cut & Curl. She's styled my hair for the past ten years. I love Teresa for her good-natured manner, even though her appearance can be disarming when you meet her. Teresa believed in experimenting with every new hair color or style on herself before offering it to a customer. Some days her hair was flaming red or orange and other days you might find her with stripes of purple among her light brown strands. Today, I saw a turquoise streak coloring her hair. She dressed younger than her forty-five years, but somehow that worked for her. Her shop was also gossip central in Meadowood. I was counting on her to know the low- down on Dickson and his extra-marital affairs.

"Hey, two of my favorite people! What are you gals up to?" asked Teresa as Colleen and I strolled into the shop.

It was a slow day; only one woman sat under a dryer and another had her head in the wash bowl as Teresa shampooed her hair and scalp. Colleen shot me a questioning look, but I shrugged and decided to go ahead. Gossip is what we came for and we were more likely to hear it with more ears to contribute. What did we have to lose? I jumped in with both feet.

"Just terrible, what happened to Mayor Dickson, isn't it? His poor wife, Adele. How's she holding up? Have you seen her lately?" I asked as I picked up a magazine and pretended to browse through the pages.

"You know, funny you ask … she was in this morning. I did her hair for her. Said she wanted a new look; got a cut and perm plus had me color her hair blond. In all these years, have you ever seen that woman other than with her drab brown hair pulled back into a bun wearing one of those old-fashioned hats with the long hat pins? I swear, you won't recognize her now."

"Wow, that is a change! What prompted the make-over?"

"Hmm, if I had to guess, I'd say she was celebrating her freedom," Teresa said as she rinsed off her customer and toweled her wet hair.

"Can you blame her?" asked the lady, eager to add her two cents, as she took the styling chair at Teresa's station. "Donald Dickson made that woman's life miserable."

"Why do you say that?" asked Colleen.

"Adele Dickson is part of my knitting circle. We meet twice a month and never were we allowed to gather at Adele's home. Her husband wouldn't allow it. And him the mayor and all. What kind of civic impression was that? Adele wasn't allowed to work outside the home or have friends over; the man practically kept her a prisoner in that big house."

"Holy cow, I would never have suspected that."

Teresa and the woman both nodded their heads. "It's true. So I say she is celebrating her freedom. Wouldn't surprise me if she puts that house on the market and moves away after the funeral," Teresa stated. She picked up a blow dryer and brush and started drying the woman's hair.

It was hard to hear over the dryer noise, but I needed to ask one more question.

"Ever hear mention of Donald having a mistress?" I shouted.

Teresa turned off the dryer and stared at me. She paused then whispered in a conspiratory manner, "Well, I heard he was cheating on his wife with a gal from Pottstown … little thing way younger than the mayor. Scandalous. But that's only hearsay. I never saw him with anyone in Meadowood, but then he wouldn't fool around in plain sight, would he?"

"Thanks, Teresa. Guess that's what I needed to know," I said. "You ladies have a nice day."

Colleen and I left the shop and stood on the sidewalk, digesting all that we had heard. I gazed down the main street and looked at all the gay banners announcing our town's bicentennial. Suddenly, I didn't feel like celebrating my little town any longer. Secret societies, a mayor who forced his wife to live as if she belonged in another century … what was going on beneath the surface of our community?

Chapter Eleven

Confession

I arranged a bucket of KFC's fried chicken onto a platter and dumped the basket of French fries out of the air fryer into a bowl. Deciding to leave the coleslaw in its container, I added it to a large tray, along with a fresh fruit salad and small bowls. I grabbed a stack of paper plates, napkins, and utensils then carried the tray out to the deck and placed it on the table. Temperatures had dropped, making the evening a pleasant time to dine al fresco.

Johnny and Billy brought out the pitcher of lemonade with ice-filled plastic tumblers. They both slid onto the picnic table bench and reached for a plate.

"This is great, Mom," Billy said. "We haven't had KFC in awhile."

Picking up my cell phone, I was just about to call Doug when I heard the kitchen door open and close. I laid down my phone as he walked out of the house and joined us on the deck.

"What's the occasion?" he asked as he took a chair and poured himself a cold drink.

"No occasion. Thought it would be fun to eat outside."

"Mmm, this looks delicious."

"I wasn't sure you'd be able to get home for dinner but I'm glad you were able to get away. After dinner, there are some things I need to talk to you about."

Doug narrowed his eyes and tried to read my expression, but I was sure he'd never guess what I wanted to question him about. It could wait until we finished eating and the boys were out of earshot.

I served everyone bowls of sliced peaches, blueberries, strawberries, and green grapes. The fresh fruit salad was a perfect complement to a summer meal. We were occupied with eating when I heard a noise at the gate then waved to my aunt to join us.

"Hey! I knocked on the door but when no one came, I thought I'd try the backyard. Looks like I'm interrupting your dinner," Fran said as she came up the deck steps.

"Have a seat and grab a plate. I've got plenty; you're just in time."

"Thanks. Maybe I'll just nibble a little," she said as she reached for a piece of fried chicken and a bowl of fruit salad.

I smiled affectionately at my aunt, such an integral part of our family. The boys finished gulping down their meal then jumped up and headed for inside.

"What's the rush?" I asked as I watched them scurry off.

"Spiderman marathon is streaming on Netflix. You said we could watch it," Johnny explained as he and Billy prepared to dash up to their room.

Doug shook his head, but stayed silent as I nodded toward the pair and grinned at my aunt.

"Sorry, Aunt Fran. Guess you know where you stand in the choice of Spiderman versus visiting with you."

Fran laughed with an indulgent smile. "How can I be angry at my god sons? I don't mind taking a back seat to an action hero."

"I'm glad you stopped by. Colleen and I did some research at the library earlier and found some interesting information that I wanted to share with you. But first, what do you know about Adele Dickson? I read a biography of our mayor and it said he married Adele Hayes and bought the pharmacy as soon as they moved to Meadowood."

"Hmm, I seem to recall that the Hayes family had wealth. It's likely that Adele brought a sizable bank account into that marriage," Aunt Fran said.

"Interesting." I glanced between Doug and Fran before bringing up what was really gnawing at me. "Remember your conversation with Ellen Ferguson?"

Fran's face took on a serious expression as she looked at me then Doug. "What did you find out?"

I turned to my husband and softly inquired, "When were you going to tell me you were a member of the Society of Free Men?"

His eyes blinked in surprise before he schooled his face in a blank expression. Doug faced me, took a sip of his drink, before asking, "How did you learn about that?"

So he didn't deny it. Okay. I laid my cards on the table. "The library has a wealth of information, including the history of the Societas Liberorum Hominum, which made for interesting reading. I also found your name on a membership list; but before that, I witnessed a secret handshake between you and Donald Dickson on debate night. Do you want to explain why you belong to this organization?"

"You're making a bigger deal out of this than is necessary. It's just a ceremonial thing. When I was promoted to sheriff, I received an honorary membership. All the town leaders belong to the society."

"I don't belong to this society and I consider myself one of the town leaders. I'm on the chamber of commerce and own a business. No one has invited me to join," Fran said with a raised eyebrow as she shot Doug an accusing look.

Doug squirmed in his seat. "I'm pretty sure you already know the society is restricted to men only. Don't shoot me; I didn't make the rules. I agree it's archaic and from colonial days."

"Well obviously, Donald Dickson was a long-term member and we've been warned that society members were working directly with Ferguson Mining to push through approval of this fracking deal. The wife of John Ferguson spoke to me and gave us the heads up on her husband's involvement with this organization," Fran stated in a firm voice.

"I learned some other interesting facts today. Did you know that Donald Dickson quite literally kept his wife Adele a prisoner in her own home? In my book, that makes her a possible suspect in his murder. The grieving widow has been celebrating her freedom around town with a complete make-over."

"Adele came into my shop yesterday and bought several new outfits, a much younger style than what she normally wears. She surprised me by her selections and when I asked her about her choices she said it was the 'new me'".

"So a woman changes her hair and clothes, I don't see a crime in that," Doug insisted. He leaned back and folded his arms across his chest.

"Well, given that her husband was cheating on her with a younger woman and his death gives her freedom to live as she wants, I think that's motive," I said with a meaningful look.

"I don't like to point fingers, but you might need to consider what Merry has said. Also the fact that Adele Dickson always wore a wide-brimmed picture hat held in place with an extremely long hat pin. Those things can be lethal. Just ask Miriam at the millinery shop; Adele was her best customer," Fran said as she matched my expression.

"Where was Adele on the day of the parade? Why wasn't she riding with Donald? Does she have an alibi?" I asked Doug. I tried to stay calm as I voiced my argument.

"I promise you both that I'll look into it. You know the spouse is normally a person of interest and receives close scrutiny; Adele is no different. I'll speak with Miriam at the hat shop too. There's a lot to consider between the mayoral campaign and this fracking business."

"Don't forget his adultery either," I said with a stern look.

A jarring ring woke me from a sound sleep as Doug reached for the telephone laying on the nightstand.

"Hello?" He asked in a groggy voice that suddenly became alert as I heard him say, "When? I'll be right there."

"What is it? What's happened?" I asked him as I sat up in bed and glanced at the clock … three-thirty. I wiped the sleep from my eyes and watched Doug jump into his clothes and splash cold water onto his face.

"Trouble at Fran's store. That's all I know."

He rushed down the stairs and out the door while I tried to make sense of who would want to harm my aunt in the middle of the night. I needed to find out.

Throwing on a pair of jeans and a t-shirt, I slipped my feet into a pair of Skechers and hurried into the boys' room down the hall.

I tapped Johnny's shoulder to wake him. He slowly opened his eyes.

"I've got to go out. You're in charge of your brother until I get back. Okay?" I whispered.

"Uh-huh," he said as he rolled over and went back to sleep.

Pressing a kiss on his cheek, I left and ran downstairs, grabbing my purse and car keys as I headed out the door. Within minutes I arrived on Park Avenue across from my aunt's shop. Doug's car and another cruiser were in front of the store. Their blue take-down lights glowed eerily in the dark night.

I spotted my aunt standing with Doug and the deputy as they inspected the broken front window of the shop. Their voices were low as they conferred over the vandalism. When they stepped to the side, I gasped as I read the slur "murderer" spray painted in red across the front door. *Oh, my goodness!*

Jumping out of my car, I ran to my aunt and wrapped my arms around her in a fierce hug. We stood staring at the damage to her shop.

"Are you okay?" I asked her.

"Of course. It's not like I was here when it happened. I'm insured. Doesn't appear to be a robbery; nothing has been stolen." She laughed and shook her head. "I was thinking about painting that door red anyway. Guess no time like the present."

I laughed with her as we held each other against the flashing blue lights and the silent night. This business with Dickson's death had taken a nasty turn.

"Tony told me he's got a sheet of plywood in his garage. We'll go get it and nail it across that window until you can get the glass replaced. I'll need you to come into the office later this morning to sign a statement, whenever it's convenient."

"Okay Doug. Thanks. Please tell Tony I said thank you too. I'll pay him for the plywood."

"No need. I'll just give it back to him after the glass is fixed."

"Aunt Fran, please come into the tea shop for breakfast this morning. I'm going to call Anna and Colleen. We need to talk. Let's get together at eight o'clock, before the shop opens so we can have a private discussion," I said.

She nodded as she surveyed the front of her shop again. "All right, I'll be along as soon as this mess is taken care of and I change my clothes."

I finally noticed her attire, a white sweater over a pair of pink pajamas and flip-flops. Definitely not her usual fashion. I swallowed back my chuckle, not wanting to add insult to injury.

"See you later then."

Crossing the empty street, I climbed back into my SUV. The milkman's truck had just started making his rounds in the wee hours of the morning as I headed home.

Sitting in my kitchen, I waited on the coffee pot to perk. I dashed off text messages to both Colleen and Anna with an emergency request for an early meeting. I mixed up a quick cheese, spinach, and bacon quiche for our breakfast and threw that in the oven to bake. Next, I got busy baking pans of streusel muffins to take into the shop. Might as well get an early start since I was up. I predicted a long day.

Chapter Twelve

Call to Action

The bell over the door chimed softly as Aunt Fran stepped into my tea shop, her face a blend of determination and concern. The warm scent of Earl Grey and freshly baked muffins filled the air. The recent break-in at Fran's store and the murder of Mayor Dickson at the bicentennial parade overshadowed the usual tranquility in my tea shop.

"Morning, Merry," Fran greeted, taking a seat at a corner table in back. "I hope you have something stronger than tea today."

"How are you doing? Did you get the broken window taken care of? I've brewed a strong pot of coffee with you in mind, Aunt Fran. I'm expecting Colleen and Anna in a minute. I think we all need to clear our heads and figure out what's going on."

Anna and Colleen arrived shortly after, their expressions just as troubled. Anna, ever the practical one, wasted no time getting to the point. "What's the emergency? Have anything to do with that hunk of plywood in front of your store?"

"Frannie's Frocks got vandalized early this morning. Did you see the door?" I asked both Colleen and Anna.

Anna nodded, her usual cheer dampened. "Do you think this is the work of a bunch of crazy Dickson supporters? Or is this a sign of someone or something more serious, like that secret society you two ran off to find?"

Colleen nodded somberly. "Merry and I did some research on the Society of Free Men at the library. According to Ellen Ferguson, they're involved with bringing fracking into our area. I don't know if they'd go to these extremes."

"Well, I never! What did you gals find out?" asked Anna.

"We learned that the men of this town, mostly businessmen and town leaders, belong to this colonial fraternal order. Gotta tell you that the member roster lists both Ron and Doug's names. Doug told me he was indoctrinated after being appointed sheriff. He swears it's ceremonial only but I can't help but wonder what kind of influence these men wield and what kind of payoff they're getting from Ferguson," I said.

"Ron told me he joined as a means to network; he thought it would help his insurance business. I'd like to think he wasn't aware of any subversive activities of the group," Colleen said.

"Hold that thought," I said as I held my hand up.

Anna and I popped into the kitchen where I sliced the quiche into portions for everyone. Balancing the tray of plates, I grabbed the coffee pot while Anna carried in a tray of tea cups and coffee mugs.

"I made breakfast for us; we should get some kind of benefit from meeting this early." I served the aromatic quiche then poured hot coffee for Fran and Anna. Earl Gray breakfast blend tea steeped in cups for Colleen and me. I'd drunk enough coffee at home while I baked to keep me wired for the rest of the day.

"You have been busy," said Colleen as she accepted the quiche.

Aunt Fran frowned. "I've never trusted Dickson, but I can't help but wonder if this society coerced him into making a deal. He didn't always act this way. Seems like it was just a few years ago when he promoted community spirit at the town Christmas celebration. That's why it doesn't make any sense to me why he'd work to harm our town now with this mining deal."

"I recall that Christmas, the sleigh rides, and the party at the Kirkland mansion. Donald Dickson twisted arms and pulled favors to make it happen. He was a different person then," I said as I sipped my tea. Memories of that eventful holiday flitted across my mind.

"So we have a break-in at Fran's store, the mayor's murder, and this secret society. There has to be a connection. What do we know for sure and what do we plan to do about it?" asked Anna.

"Leave it up to the sheriff?" suggested Colleen.

"Since when do we ever avoid getting involved?" I asked with a smirk. I felt it was my civic duty to defend my community, despite my husband's best efforts to keep me out of his investigations.

We all sat silently mulling over the problem when suddenly a loud tapping on the shop's door interrupted our reverie. I looked toward the door and spotted Trixie Jones with her face pressed against the glass, peering into the shop.

"It's that pesky reporter," I told the others as I walked toward the door. Unlocking the door, I kept the chain latched and opened it a few inches. "Come back at ten when we're open."

Trixie shifted back and forth, shuffling her feet and tried to look past me. "Is that Fran Andrews in the back? I wanted to speak to her about the break-in at her store. Please, can I have a few minutes?"

"Are you proposing a real interview or do you plan on writing more libelous lies?"

"I'm sorry about that first article. I mean it. Can I please ask her about the vandalism? This story is taking some serious turns and I mean to write about it," Trixie said with more honesty than I'd heard before.

I considered her anxious expression then slid the door closed enough to remove the chain then allowed her to enter. She followed me quietly toward our secluded table. I noticed she glanced around the shop as we walked.

"Nice place you have; I've always meant to stop in," Trixie commented. "Good morning, ladies. I'm sorry to interrupt your breakfast but I wonder if you'd permit me a couple questions."

"Would you like a slice of quiche? I've got some left in the kitchen," I offered.

"Really? Mmm, yeah, that'd be great. Smells good."

I left to plate the last slice of quiche, warmed it briefly in the microwave, then served it to the nervous reporter. "Coffee or tea? Slide that chair up and squeeze in."

"I'll, uh, have a coffee please. This tastes delicious. Thanks," Trixie said as she ate a bite of the egg dish.

We all resumed eating our breakfast; an awkward silence filled the air. I studied Trixie. Glancing over at Fran, she nodded slightly, reading my mind as she always did.

"So, Trixie, what I want to know is ... how serious are you about writing an honest story about what's really happening? There's a bigger story than just Donald Dickson's murder. Can you help investigate with us? It'll be a scoop no other reporter will have."

Trixie's eyes widened. She stared at me then Fran; her mouth hung open. "Seriously? Just give me a chance! Oh boy. I had a feeling, you know? Clue me in. What's going on? You gals are in the middle of everything that goes on in this town. I can tell. What do you need me to do?"

I smiled at her. Where to start?

"Guess we need to finish our breakfast first before it gets cold. Then you need to listen to a story that may surprise you."

"Okay, so now you know everything that we do. We can pursue the local members of S.O.F.M. because we live around them; they're part of our town and we see these guys daily. What we need you to do is interview John Ferguson. I think he'd talk to you as a reporter more so than any of us. He knows there are hostile feelings here but you can give him a chance to tell his side of the story. Ask him what the company plans are now that Mayor Dickson is dead. Did Ferguson get a signed agreement from Dickson or is that still up for negotiation with the town? Dig around but don't antagonize. Can you do that?" I asked Trixie.

Trixie scribbled furiously in her notepad.

"Yeah, I sure can. We need to find out more about the S.O.F.M. If they were involved in Fran's break-in and the mayor's murder, we need proof. Hey! What about Dickson's wife and girlfriend … any chance we have a love triangle?"

I laughed out loud. "Did you ever see Donald Dickson? He wasn't exactly Brad Pitt handsome. Hard to believe two women would fight over him."

"Well, it's still an angle," Anna chimed in. "But you've got a point."

I checked the time on my watch. "Okay ladies. You've each got your assignments. Anna and I've got to get this cleaned up and prepare to open the shop for the day."

Aunt Fran laid a hand on my arm to pause me before I dashed into the kitchen. "Do you think Johnny would be interested in painting the store's front door? I'd pay him, of course. He's old enough now to take on a serious project. I'd really like to get that slur covered up today."

"I'll ask him. I'm sure he'd want to help."

"Great. Tell him to come over after he's had his breakfast. I'm going to leave here and go buy some red paint."

Chapter Thirteen

Society Snoop

"What else did he say?" I questioned Colleen as she hopped onto one of my kitchen bar stools. I slid a glass of iced tea toward her and a plate of oatmeal cookies that I had baked earlier.

"You know, I've never seen Ron so flustered. He just stood there staring and debating with himself about how much he was able to tell me. The poor man, if you could have seen his face! I don't mind telling you, I had to swallow to keep from laughing. I didn't want to hurt his feelings, but when I reminded him that as his wife I had the right to know where he spent his evenings ... well, he caved."

"I can just imagine. So did Ron tell you where this great secret man's club was held?"

"Yes, he did. Did you know that there are large rooms on the second floor above the Meadowood Apothecary? Evidently, Donald Dickson offered to rent that space to the S.O.F.M some years back as its official meeting hall. According to Ron, they meet once a month on the second Tuesday of the month at eight p.m."

My eyes flew to the calendar hanging on my kitchen wall. "Wait a minute ... that's today. I mean, this is the second Tuesday of the month. We've got to get in there and have a look around. Oh, to be a fly on the wall tonight. Do you think they'll still hold the meeting without Dickson?" I asked, as an idea percolated in my mind.

"Pretty sure. Ron told me he planned on attending. Seemed to be a relief to him now that I knew where he'd be and no more secrets between us. What are you thinking? You've got that look in your eye and it usually means trouble."

"We've got to investigate. What if there was a fight between the members about this fracking business and someone decided to swing the vote their way by eliminating Dickson? I'd really like to hear what these men had planned and who was working with Ferguson."

"There's a back door and set of stairs that go up. Ron told me the door is unlocked one hour before the meeting begins, to allow members access," Colleen stated.

"We need to slip in before that and check the place out. Let's meet behind Aunt Fran's shop at say, six-thirty. The pharmacy is just across the street and we can dash over."

"All right, but we better not get caught," sighed Colleen.

"C'mon, we're doing this for the good of the community. We need to save Meadowood from corporate swindling and the destruction of our environment."

"You make us sound like crusaders," laughed Colleen.

"Ha, give me a minute and I'll drag out my wonder woman cape!"

We parked around the corner on the side street since Colleen's bright yellow Mustang stuck out like a neon light. I pulled in behind her and we hurried down the street and crept behind the pharmacy building. A plain wooden door, undistinguishable with no markings, stood against the back of the structure, off-center on the wall.

"Here, put these on," I said as I handed Colleen a pair of surgical rubber gloves and pulled on my own.

"Where'd you get these?" Colleen asked with a raised eyebrow but complied in my request.

"Bought a box when the scouts were staining those wooden book racks last Christmas. They come in handy. We don't want our fingerprints to be found."

Approaching the door, I hastily looked around and jiggled the doorknob. Locked. I reached into a pocket of my purse and pulled out a plastic card. Sliding the hard plastic into the doorframe and lock assembly, I guided it up and down a fraction until I heard a click.

"How did you learn to do that?" Colleen whispered as we slipped into the building and eased the door shut.

I locked the door behind us. "Saw it on a Hallmark mystery movie. I didn't want to risk breaking off a good credit card so I thought this old gas station rewards card would work. Glad it did. C'mon, let's get upstairs and check this place out."

"Are you sure about this? Breaking and entering does not look good on my resume."

Dashing up the stairs, we entered a wide-open room with three doors set along the adjacent walls. The massive space contained rows of typical meeting room chairs with a speaker's lectern facing them. A long conference table, covered in a faded gold cloth, sat beneath a purple satin banner proclaiming Society of Free Men in Latin. The table held a unique set of triple candleholders, a trikirion, one placed on each end of the table. A huge leather-bound book, its gold-leaf lettering worn smooth on spine and cover, lay in a place of honor on the center of the table. I couldn't decipher the name on the book.

"Wow, the only time I saw a candle holder like that was in an art history book," I whispered.

There didn't appear to be anything else to see in the room beyond the contents on that table, so I decided to explore the other doors. Opening the door in the far corner, I found a small powder room, furnished with an antique wash basin standing on four legs that probably dated back to when the building first got indoor plumbing. Shutting the door, I moved on to the next door further down the wall.

Colleen eased the door open; the dark room appeared to hold storage shelves. Cobwebs brushed my face as I stepped into the closet; my hands quickly swiped them away. We moved forward and pulled a chain hanging from the ceiling. A single light bulb lit the dim space. Dusty boxes of Christmas decorations and old advertising displays, along with various supplies, filled the shelves.

"Seems like a lot of junk Donald chose to store up here. Nothing important from the looks of it."

We stepped out of the closet and turned the light off.

"One more door to open. I feel like we're in a game show; what's behind door number three?" Colleen said.

"What time do you have? We better hurry before someone arrives."

Just as we started to peek behind the third door, I heard voices on the stairs. Colleen and I exchanged a fleeting look of panic, then ran back to the dark storage room and jumped inside. We both held our breaths as the voices grew louder and footsteps sounded on the wooden floor of the meeting room. Chairs scraped the floor as men took seats and talked among themselves. Unless they took a break and everyone left the room, we were stuck for the duration. If we were caught, there was no way I could explain to Doug what we were doing there. It would appear that I was getting my wish to be the fly on the wall.

"What are we going to do?" Colleen whispered as she clutched my arm.

"Wait. What else can we do? Maybe we'll hear something good."

"Ron's going to kill me," she whispered in a strangled voice.

"Don't you start crying," I warned her.

"I'm not." But I heard her sniffle and knew my friend was holding back tears at our dilemma.

The voices in the room grew louder and I could tell the meeting was about to begin when I heard a gavel hammering. Placing my ear against the door, I leaned on it to listen better. The door creaked. I froze. Did anyone hear that? I eased my weight off the flimsy panel and held my breath again. No footsteps approached our hiding place. I think we were safe.

Chairs scraped again as the men stood and a chorus of voices rose as they recited some pledge then resumed their seats. A stronger voice rose above the murmurs in the room. I strained to listen and identify the speaker. Did I dare to peek? The closet was along the back wall, behind the rows of chairs. Maybe if I could just crack the door enough …

Colleen grabbed my hand on the doorknob and shook her head vehemently. I paused.

"What?!" I hissed.

"Are you crazy?"

"Shush. I wanna hear better and see who's talking."

I inched the door open a crack. Putting my face to the door, I could see through the crack with my left eye but only one side of the room. The speaker started addressing the assembly. I concentrated on the voice.

"It sounds like Kevin Wyatt is talking," I whispered to Colleen.

Wyatt had moved into Meadowood and took over the management of the local savings and loan after its previous manager had been arrested for embezzlement. Geez, that place sure hired some losers. I'm glad I did my banking business with the commercial bank in town, not the savings and loan.

Colleen and I both pressed our ears to the door. Luckily, the flimsy panel didn't block most sounds and voices weren't too distorted. We were both surprised by the speaker's next remarks.

"John Ferguson needs reassurance from the town leaders of Meadowood before he'll go ahead with his project. As businessmen, you know what this means. More revenue, more money in your pocket with no personal outlay. As Vice-President of the S.O.F.M., now that Don has passed, we owe it to his memory to decide this matter. Don't let those environmental nuts and green protesters stop progress."

Someone stood up. I could only see his back. I wished I knew who it was. He directed his comments to the assembled group.

"Think before you vote, men. Even Donald Dickson had second thoughts and was wavering on his decision to allow mining outside our town. I'm sure if he were here tonight, he'd vote no. Yeah, I know, those environmental nuts are throwing all kinds of numbers and facts at us, but some of that stuff makes sense. Once we go down that road, there's no going back. I vote no on the journey." He sat down and crossed his arms as he waited on the response to his words.

Colleen and I exchanged looks of wonder. Did Dickson object to the mining deal? Was he killed because of his opposition? His comments at the debate appeared to be at odds with that premise, but thinking back, he did only admit to a study being made and not actual negotiations with Ferguson. I could well imagine that a lot of money was riding on this contract. Was it worth killing over?

Kevin Wyatt's voice addressed the room. I could hear mumbles and side conversations among the members.

"All right, quiet down please. By a show of hands, how many are in favor of negotiating with Ferguson Mining Company to lease Meadowood land?"

A dozen hands or more raised on the left side of the room, but I couldn't see enough through the crack to know how many more voted yes on the other side of the room. A sinking feeling settled in the bottom of my stomach at the thought of our wonderful community being destroyed.

"Show of hands please, how many are against the Ferguson deal?"

Sounds of chairs scraping wood as men jumped up; hands raised proudly. I almost shoved the door open so I could see the count but had to pray the chairperson would announce the outcome. Colleen and I waited anxiously.

A cheer went up in the room. Men clapped each other on the back then filed out of the room. What was the vote? Who won? We listened for more voices, some announcement, but heard none. After fifteen more minutes, we decided it was safe to sneak out of the closet. I peeked around the open door at the empty room. Colleen and I hurried down the stairs and out the back door.

Embers from a lit cigarette glowed in the dark shadows of the connecting alley, unnoticed by the two women in their haste to escape.

"Do you think Ron attended?" I asked Colleen as we stood next to our cars.

"I'm not sure; he said he planned to. I didn't hear his voice. Should I tell him we were there?"

"Heavens no! You'll learn that sometimes it's better if the husband doesn't know everything. Helps to keep peace in the marriage that way. I'm not saying to lie, just don't always tell the complete truth," I said with a laugh. "Doug would have a heart attack if he knew half the stuff I got into. C'mon, we better go. Let's get together with Anna and Fran at her store tomorrow. Maybe Trixie will have some news too."

Chapter Fourteen

R.I.P.

As soon as we closed the tea shop for the day, Anna and I walked down the street to meet Colleen and Aunt Fran in the back of her store. Colleen stood chatting with Betty at the counter when we entered the dress shop through the newly painted deep red portal. A swag of pink hydrangea blooms decorated the door. Two men balanced a large pane of glass as they sought to replace the broken front window. The mannequin, vacated from the front window display, laid in the corner next to the register with a pile of clothing and accessories on the floor. She waited to resume her position of glory.

I browsed the new merchandise as I made my way back to the employee break room. Couldn't help myself as I passed the pretty new tops and dresses. My aunt poured herself a cup of coffee then joined the three of us at a small corner table.

"Well? What did the two of you get into last night?" she asked, her gaze focused on me and Colleen.

"We attended a meeting of the Society of Free Men last night," I said and waited for her reaction.

Anna snorted her drink of water at my outrageous statement, coughing as it went down the wrong way.

"All day long, you kept that tidbit to yourself. You could have told me before this," Anna drawled, miffed at being kept in the dark.

"They let you in, just like that?" asked Fran. Her voice reflected her skepticism.

"Not exactly. We sort of let ourselves in ahead of the meeting and then got trapped in a storage closet while it went on. Made for some interesting listening," I admitted.

"Oh my goodness!" Anna exclaimed. "One of these days y'all going to regret the risks you take."

"What did you learn? Hope it was worth your caper," Fran asked us as she took another sip of her coffee.

"For starters, Kevin Wyatt from the S&L has taken over leadership of the group. Get this ... he said Donald Dickson had postponed negotiating with Ferguson and had second thoughts about the mining deal. He called for a vote among the members to approve going forward with the plan," I stated.

"Really? That surprises me. I thought Donald was gungho to bring in fracking," Fran said.

"I don't know. They did a show of hands and I could only see one side of the room from where we were hiding. There was a bunch of applause but Kevin didn't announce the decision. You have no idea how annoyed I felt not knowing."

Colleen spoke up in her soft voice, "Ron attended. I haven't figured out a way to bring up the subject yet, but I should be able to find out what the vote decision was by tonight."

I grinned and squeezed her hand. "I'm sure you'll think of something, being newlyweds yet. So ... either Dickson wanted to back out and someone in the Society killed him to keep the deal, or someone wanted to stop Ferguson and killed the mayor to prevent the mining contract thinking Dickson was in favor of it. Either way, there could be a guilty party directing the outcome. I don't know if we're any closer to discovering who killed the mayor."

"Don't forget he was fooling around on Adele," Anna reminded us.

"Hell hath no fury like a woman scorned," she quoted and wagged her finger before us.

"True. It wouldn't be the first time a man was killed over unfaithfulness. We should try and learn the name of the gal he had on the side," Fran said.

"Reverend Kilgore stopped into the tea shop this morning. He mentioned Adele is holding calling hours at Wagner's tonight and he will perform the private funeral service for the mayor tomorrow. Are we all going to the viewing tonight?" I asked.

"Of course. We're business owners and should pay respects to our mayor. What time?" Fran asked.

"I think it starts at seven. There's bound to be a huge turnout. Parking will be at a premium. Maybe Anna and I can ride together. Doug will likely be on duty and already at the funeral home."

"Send the boys over to my house and Chuck can stay home with them. I'm sure Chuck will appreciate not having to attend another funeral gathering," Anna said.

"Okay, sounds like a plan. I'll pick you up a little before seven and drop off my guys. We'll meet the two of you at the funeral home. Colleen, do you think Ron will go?"

"Like Fran said, he's a business owner so it's only proper that he show up for the mayor. We'll both be there. I'll meet you at the entrance; Ron can shmooze with his buddies."

"I'm eager to hear from that reporter as to what she learned from Ferguson. Wonder if it matches what you heard at the meeting," Fran said.

"Hmm, me too. See everyone later. Guess I better get home and fix dinner for my gang before this thing tonight."

Wagner's Funeral Home was located in a prominent Victorian structure painted an ominous gray with black trimmed windows, and complete with turrets and gables on its three-story high roof. It had once been home to a wealthy investor in the late 1800s. Like many immense older homes, they were impossible to heat or cool and wound up being sold for some type of commercial use. The gothic-designed house could be spooky enough in daylight, but at night, it seemed like a place straight out of a Stephen King novel. The only thing missing was a gargoyle atop one of the gables. As I had expected, the lot was full, and I had to drive the block twice before finding a spot to park along the street.

The somber atmosphere at Wagner's was almost suffocating as I stepped inside with Anna. Aunt Fran and Colleen waited near the entrance. The familiar scent of lilies and polished wood hung in the air, but today, there was something different—a strange tension that seemed to hum just beneath the surface of the usual grief.

Aunt Fran walked beside me, her expression somber. As we entered the parlor, I couldn't help but notice the way people glanced around, their eyes not just sad, but curious, even wary. Meadowood's tight-knit community was used to gathering for occasions like this, but the sudden death of Mayor Donald Dickson had shaken our small town to its core. Everyone present seemed to sense that this was more than just a farewell —it was the closing of a chapter that had left too many questions unanswered.

Anna and Colleen followed close behind, both wearing appropriate black dresses. I glanced down at my own simple navy blue skirt and jacket, feeling slightly under-dressed considering the circumstances. We'd come together to pay our respects to Adele Dickson, the mayor's widow, but I knew we were also here to observe and identify anyone or thing suspicious.

The room was filled with Meadowood's familiar faces, though today they were marked by grief. There was Mr. Harper, the stern town council member, standing rigidly by the door, his eyes scanning the room as if he could keep his emotions at bay through sheer force of will. Near the front, I spotted Georgia Simmons, clutching her hand-kerchief like a lifeline as she dabbed at her eyes. Retired sheriff Edgar

Simmons stood next to his wife. The local florists had clearly outdone themselves, with towering arrangements of white lilies and roses framing the dark walnut casket, where Donald Dickson lay in peaceful repose.

As we moved through the room, offering brief nods of acknowledgment to the other mourners, I felt a tug at my sleeve. Colleen leaned in close, her voice barely above a whisper. "This place gives me the creeps, Merry. It's so quiet, and everyone looks ... I don't know, almost scared."

I nodded slightly, understanding her unease. There was something unsettling about the atmosphere, something that made the hairs on the back of my neck stand on end. "Know what you mean, it's not just grief," I murmured. "There's something else here. Everyone feels it."

Aunt Fran's hand tightened around her purse as we approached Adele near the casket. Teresa was right. I barely recognized the transformed woman. She appeared ten years younger. Adele, once a mousy, meek woman who barely spoke above a whisper, stood before us with a confidence I'd never seen in her before. Her brown, unremarkable hair was now a striking shade of blonde, styled in soft curls that framed her face. A simple but elegant black dress hugged her figure, replacing her plain unassuming wardrobe. Adele's makeup was expertly applied to highlight her attractive features. Stunning. She wore a solemn expression, showing the appropriate amount of grief for a widow, yet with a quiet undertone that made me pause.

Adele stood alone. Her daughter was absent from her own father's funeral. How odd.

"Merry, Fran, Anna, and Colleen," Adele greeted each of us, her voice steady, almost detached. It was as if she had shed not just her old appearance, but her entire demeanor along with it.

"Adele," I said gently, offering her a small smile. "We're so sorry for your loss."

She gave a brief nod, her eyes scanning our faces. "Thank you. It's been ... difficult. But I'm managing."

Managing? The word seemed oddly clinical, almost cold, given the circumstances. I exchanged a quick glance with Aunt Fran, who looked equally taken aback. This was not the Adele we knew.

"Adele," Aunt Fran said gently, reaching out to take her hand. "You have my deepest sympathies."

Adele looked up, her blue eyes clear. She dabbed a lace handkerchief to the corner of a dry eye. "Thank you, Fran," she replied in a steady voice. "It means a lot that you're here, even if you were Donald's opponent."

"You understand, that's just politics, not personal," Fran replied.

I stepped forward, feeling a lump form in my throat; funerals always affected me. I searched for the right words. "Donald was … he was a good man. He'll be missed by everyone in Meadowood."

Adele nodded, squeezing my hand briefly before letting go. "Thank you, Merry. He thought highly of you, you know. Always said you had a good head on your shoulders."

I managed a small smile. "Thank you. That's kind of you to say."

Anna and Colleen offered their condolences as well, their voices soft and respectful. As we stood there, the weight of the moment pressing down on us, I couldn't help but notice the way Adele's gaze drifted toward the casket, a flicker of something unreadable passing over her face.

After a few moments of silence, Aunt Fran spoke up again. "Adele, if there's anything you need—anything at all—please don't hesitate to ask. We're all here for you."

Adele's lips curved into a sad smile. "Thank you, Fran. It's just … it's all so sudden. I still can't believe he's gone."

My eyes flicked to Fran, and I raised my eyebrows at the widow's melodramatic statement.

I glanced around the room, taking in the other mourners. There were the usual occupants—town officials, local business owners, and long-time residents. But there were also a few unfamiliar faces, people I didn't recognize. One man in particular, standing off to the side with his hands clasped in front of him, caught my attention.

He was tall and thin, with graying hair and a sharp, almost predatory look about him. His eyes fixed on Adele, though he made no move to approach her. I noticed a young woman, wearing that bloom of youth only someone twenty-something wore, with a tear-streaked face standing near the man. I wondered about their identities.

"Adele," I began cautiously, "I know this might not be the best time, but ... do you know if Donald had any enemies? Anyone who might have wanted to hurt him?"

Adele's eyes widened slightly, and she looked at me with a mix of surprise and confusion. "Enemies? No, I don't think so. Donald was well-liked, respected even. I told the sheriff the same."

I hesitated, glancing at Aunt Fran, who gave me a small nod of encouragement. "It's just ... the way everything happened. Donald's death at the parade then the break-in at Fran's store ... it seems like too much of a coincidence."

Adele's expression darkened, and she shook her head slowly. "I didn't hear about the store break in. Sorry. I don't know, Merry. It all seems so unreal. But if there was something going on, Donald never told me about it."

Colleen leaned in, her voice low and serious. "Did Donald ever mention anything about the Society of Free Men? We've heard some things ... things that make us wonder if they might be involved."

Adele's face went pale, and for a moment, she looked like she might faint. She quickly regained her composure, but the fear in her eyes was unmistakable.

"The Society?" she whispered. "I ... I don't know anything about them. Donald never talked about his business or friends with me. But I think he was worried about something, more than just the election."

My heart raced. "Why?"

Adele shook her head again, more vigorously this time. "I don't know, Merry. It was more a feeling I had watching him. I overheard him on the phone once, he said '*they*' had too much influence in town.

Perhaps the *'they'* he referred to was the Society. He never confided in me."

I exchanged a glance with Aunt Fran, who looked just as troubled as I felt. There was definitely something more going on here, something that Donald Dickson had been involved with before his death. Maybe the Ferguson mining deal?

Colleen spoke up. "Mrs. Dickson, did Donald keep any records at home? Notes, files—anything that might help us understand what he was working on?"

Adele hesitated, her gaze drifting to the floor as she thought. "He had a study at home. He was always so meticulous, keeping notes on everything. If there's anything, it would be there."

Aunt Fran placed a comforting hand on Adele's shoulder. "Would you mind if we took a look? We just want to help, Adele. If there's something there that can explain what happened, we need to find it."

Adele looked up at us, her eyes filled with a mixture of hope and fear. "Shouldn't the sheriff be examining his files? My husband's papers are private. I don't know what good you could do."

"I promise we won't disclose anything private that could harm his reputation as the town's long-term mayor. We just want to learn if his association with the Society put him in danger."

She nodded slowly. "Alright. Come around tomorrow and I'll give you the key to the study."

As we left Adele's side, I couldn't shake the feeling that we were walking into something much bigger than we'd anticipated. There was something in her eyes—something guarded, maybe even a little defiant —that made me feel like we were missing a piece of the puzzle.

The tension in the room seemed to grow as we moved through the crowd, and I caught a few curious glances from the other mourners as if they knew we were up to something.

Outside, the sun sank on the horizon, casting long shadows across the pavement as we made our way to my SUV. The evening air felt cool, a stark contrast to the suffocating atmosphere inside the funeral home.

"Well, that was ... intense," Colleen said, breaking the silence as we approached my car. Her car was parked on the next block near Fran's.

"No kidding," Anna replied.

"I think the merry widow is lying," Fran said in a surprise statement.

"Hmm, you think she was aware of her husband's business," I stated. "I got that feeling too. She's hiding something."

"Merry, do you really think the Society is involved?" Anna asked.

I nodded slowly, still processing everything we'd learned. "I don't know for sure, but it's starting to seem that way. Maybe digging through the mayor's papers tomorrow will shed light on the problem. I wish we knew what the outcome of that vote was that Colleen and I had witnessed. I can't wait to hear what Ron has to say. Hopefully, Trixie can fill in the gaps from her interview with John Ferguson too."

Aunt Fran cautioned us as I climbed into my SUV, her expression grim. "We need to be careful, girls. This has gone beyond politics. It's become dangerous."

I watched them as Fran and Colleen met Ron then walked toward their waiting vehicles.

As we drove away, my mind raced with possibilities. The quiet streets of Meadowood seemed to hold their breath, as if waiting for the storm that was surely coming. And I knew, deep down, that we were heading straight into the heart of it.

Chapter Fifteen

Adele

Rain poured and dark clouds filled the sky, making it a very gloomy and depressive day. I flipped pancakes on the griddle and took strips of bacon out of the microwave for Billy and Johnny's breakfast. Rainy days in the summer were no fun at all for active boys.

"What are you guys going to do today?"

"I dunno. Maybe we'll go over to Stevie's and play video games. We had planned to take our bikes to Fox Run Park and hit the trails, but that's not gonna happen. Not with all this rain. Tomorrow won't be good either even if it's sunny because of all the mud. Guess we'll have to wait a couple days," Johnny said, his chin propped in his palm as he watched the raindrops hit the windows.

Billy grabbed another piece of bacon. He started speaking with a full mouth as he chewed the crisp meat. "Can we hang out with Stevie? There's nothing to do at home."

"Don't talk with your mouth full. Yes, it's okay with me as long as Mrs. Thompson says you can."

"Aww, you know she'll say it's okay."

"Yes, but be polite and ask first. Call Stevie and check with his mother please."

I poured a fresh cup of coffee and flipped a single pancake onto a plate for my breakfast. I didn't dare consume as many calories as my boys did or I'd be twice my size. Oh, to be young again and not have to worry about what you ate. Guess that train's left the station.

Doug entered the kitchen, grabbed a piece of bacon off Billy's plate then filled a thermos bottle with hot coffee.

"Planning on being out of the office today?" I asked as I watched him.

"Yeah, maybe. What's your day look like?" he asked.

"Same-o-same-o. Open the tea shop at ten, serve the lunch crowd then meet Aunt Fran in the afternoon to visit Adele Dickson at her house." I waited for my words to sink in and the explosion they'd cause.

Doug's hand paused in midair as he reached for his coffee. "What did you say? Why are you visiting Adele Dickson? You better not be running a shadow investigation."

"She invited us," I answered him with an innocent smile on my face.

"Uh-huh. When was this?"

"At the funeral home last night. She asked us to stop over. We're just being neighborly. You know I've worked with the mayor in the past and so has Aunt Fran, even if she was running against him now. What's wrong with paying a call to his widow?"

"Nothing's wrong. It's just that I know you, Meredith Gardner, and I can tell when you're up to something. Please don't make this case more difficult." Doug ran his fingers through his hair, brushing a stray lock off his forehead. He jammed his hat on and reached for his gear. Doug turned and gave me a defeated look before heading out into the rain.

Business had been slow during the day. The rain kept folks at home and not browsing the shops downtown. I turned the lock and placed the closed sign in the window at two o'clock.

"I hope Chuck was able to get some work done today with the boys there," I said as I wiped off tables and straightened merchandise on shelves.

"I'm sure he managed. He told me he had planned to work from home on a couple reports. Believe me, he can tune out voices and noise when he works. He certainly tunes out my voice when I'm trying to talk to him," Anna said with a laugh.

"Do you mind finishing closing up the shop? I need to meet Aunt Fran; we promised Adele we'd be there by three."

"No, you go ahead and run along. We're almost done here. I just need to empty the till and make a bank deposit. We did pretty good this week. I think our profits are up at least fifteen percent," Anna remarked.

"That's what I like to hear. I'll be able to pay off Aunt Fran earlier than I had promised if business keeps doing so well. Maybe we should think about doing a back-to-school special next month ... treat all those weary mothers doing school shopping. Something to think about."

"Hmm, sounds like a good idea. I'll play around with some ideas. You better run," Anna said as she glanced at the clock.

"Okay. Thanks. See you later. I'll tell you all about our visit with the merry widow."

I drove the two blocks to my aunt's store and beeped the horn out front. She came running out, dodging raindrops, when she spotted my car. As soon as she was settled in the passenger seat, I pulled away and headed toward the Dickson home located on Birch Court, about two miles away.

"Wow, impressive!" I said as we turned into the upscale neighborhood. "I've never been on this side of town. Always wanted to see how the other half lived." Driving slowly, we gazed at the selection of extraordinary homes with their tall columns, porticos, and expansive circular driveways that lined the cul-de-sac street.

"Pushing pills must pay well," commented Aunt Fran.

"Evidently. What do you think these homes are worth?" I asked.

"At least a million; way beyond my pay grade," Fran said.

We read house numbers as I crept along then stopped before a huge home that I could only classify as a mansion.

"This is the place ... 454 Birch."

A red brick structure rose three-stories with a pair of dormer windows set into a gray slate roof. On each side of the central building, lower one-and-a-half-story wings spread out. Black shutters framed the tall windows. Manicured landscaping graced the foundation and among artfully planted flower beds behind stone retaining walls. I speculated that the home sat on at least a half acre of land. Donald Dickson definitely lived well, or at least he did.

We pulled up into the drive and I parked near the front entrance, where we could dash under the portico roof and out of the rain. I pressed the doorbell and listened to a melodious chime inside the house. An older woman, wearing a gray maid's uniform and a white apron, opened the door.

"Yes? May I help you?" she asked.

"Hello. Fran Andrews and Meredith Gardner. We have an appointment to see Mrs. Dickson," I said as I stole a glance inside the wide foyer.

"Of course. Please come this way."

We stepped into the palatial entry onto dark, gleaming hardwood floors with a round Persian rug covering the center of the area. A rich burgundy framed a myriad of vivid colors in the rug's intricate pattern. A heavy console table sat on the rug holding a fluted crystal vase filled with white roses. I wondered if the flowers had come from the funeral. Next to the vase, a wide-brimmed silk hat lay on the table; a long, lethal hat pin protruded from the brim.

A sparkling chandelier hung high above the entry. A creamy-colored wallpaper with a tiny white-on-white marquis design covered the walls. The home's elegant appearance was meant to instantly impress the occasional visitor with the owner's wealth or importance. Yet, it seemed odd that Donald never allowed Adele to host friends in the home. Made me ponder just who Donald did intend to impress.

Adele descended the long staircase, gliding one hand along the balustrade as the grand lady of the manor. She resembled Barbara Stanwyck in *Double Indemnity,* and I instantly wondered why my mind jumped to that femme fatale image. Adele greeted us regally as we waited in the foyer. She still wore her black dress from the morning's burial service. Her blond hair and makeup appeared perfect, no tear stains. Once again, I was struck with the amazing change in Adele's appearance. The mouse had vanished and a queen had been born.

"Hello Fran and Merry. Please come into the sitting room." She waved her hand to indicate one of the doors on the left then turned to the servant. "Mildred, please bring a tray of refreshments for my guests. Thank you."

Fran and I stepped into a cheerful room with buttery yellow walls and white satin draperies. Landscape paintings adorned the walls and fragrant flowers filled several vases around the room. It was a decidedly feminine room. I noted the selection of books and reading materials that filled a short bookcase and a forgotten, half-finished cross stitch sampler tossed onto an end table.

The maid carried a tray into the room and placed it on the center of the oval cherry wood table positioned between the pair of facing brocade sofas. The tray held an assortment of cookies and pastries that I recognized from Martha's bakery, plus a pitcher of lemonade and three tall glasses filled with ice.

"Ladies. Help yourself, please," Adele said, as she waved her hand toward the offering.

"Thank you. Everything looks wonderful," I said as I poured a glass of lemonade and handed it to my aunt then poured another for myself. "Can I get one for you, Adele?"

"No thank you. I'm still quite full from the luncheon that followed the service earlier."

We sat back and sipped our drinks; an awkward silence settled between us. I gave my aunt the side-eye and nodded toward the widow.

Fran cleared her throat. The small noise appeared to startle Adele from her silent musings.

"Um, Adele, perhaps you'd like to show us into Donald's study? You said we could read some of his papers and I don't want to impose on your time. I'm sure you've had a difficult day as it is." Fran made to stand, setting her glass on the tray.

"Oh, yes. Of course. Silly of me. Donald's study is in the east wing. He always enjoyed the morning sun shining on his desk. It's this way," Adele said as she moved in a dream-like state down a short hallway and opened a pair of massive mahogany doors into a study. Floor to ceiling bookcases spanned two walls creating a library that I itched to browse. Dark hunter green walls surrounded a bank of windows that opened onto a brick patio. Donald's desk resembled something belonging in a law office and faced the expansive window. Matching wooden file cabinets and office equipment were placed along the wall behind the desk. A thick Aubusson rug graced the hardwood floors. A tan leather sofa faced the windows, flanked by a pair of comfortable hunter green club chairs. If the sitting room reflected Adele, then this room most certainly reflected a man's taste.

"All I ask, is that you put things back where you found them when you're done. You're welcome to search his files and papers on the desk or cabinets." Adele turned and left the room.

"All right." Turning to my aunt, I asked, "Where do you want to begin?"

"I'll start with the desk top and you go through the file cabinet," Fran said.

"What are we looking for exactly?"

"Anything pertaining to Ferguson and that mining deal for starters. If you see anything else that looks odd, pull it out."

We got to work. Minutes ticked by. The only sound being the rustle of paper. I opened the top drawer of the short cabinet and peeked at file folders and scanned documents, finding records of personal purchases and expenses relating to the house. I tucked that file back into the folder and moved to the next. All I found was more of the same. I closed the drawer and opened the one below.

Riffling through the file folders, I found records that pertained more to the town of Meadowood and his position as mayor. It appeared Donald had moved his archived city records to his home files as I read the older dates on documents.

"Shouldn't the city keep documents pertaining to city business? Why did the mayor have them in his personal files?" I asked my aunt as I continued my search.

Pulling out a second folder and skimming the first document, I whistled softly as I removed it from the file and waved it at my aunt.

"I've got a lease. Look at this." I handed her the legal paper. "Colleen and I heard Kevin Wyatt discuss a lease that the society planned to negotiate with Ferguson Mining. What do you think?"

Fran studied the terms of the lease then handed it back to me. "Just a second ... Where is it? I just had my hand on a small map." She moved some papers on the desk top then triumphantly removed an obviously hand-drawn map. "Here, check this out."

Fran spread the map on the desk surface and we leaned over it, reading the markers and penciled descriptions. I compared it to the legal description of land mentioned on the lease.

"Wait a minute! Does this look like the tract of land near Fox Run Park where our scouts hold their annual jamboree? See that property line? That's the Granger Farm ... well it's part of OSU's agricultural program now, but that's it," I said.

"Please don't tell me that Ferguson Mining intends to run their fracking operation this close to our town and next to a recreational area. This would be disastrous. Worse than I thought. What names are on that lease?" Fran asked as she grabbed the document for a closer look. She turned several pages of the lease, zeroing in on the last page with signature lines. Blank. No signatures ... just typed names: John Ferguson, Mayor Donald Dickson, and Woodland Design, LLC.

"Is this a copy before all parties signed it?" I asked as I studied the paper.

"I don't know. You said Kevin Wyatt told his members that the deal still needed approval and another member said Dickson had second thoughts. Who do you think is the owner of that tract of land? The lease only names a limited liability company. Whoever it is would stand to gain a lot of revenue from this deal." Fran held the document as her mind spun.

"Wouldn't a search online provide the owners of that liability company? Anna and I had to register our names and LLC when we opened the tea shop. I should be able to track down whoever is behind this so-called Woodland Design. Probably a society member too, or they wouldn't be pushing so hard to make the deal."

"Let's keep these. Adele won't need these papers and if they're only copies, the originals are likely in some attorney's office." Fran folded the map and lease then slipped them into her purse.

"I think we've seen enough," I said. I closed the file drawer and Fran straightened up the papers on top the desk.

"Unless Donald Dickson owned the deed to that property, I don't imagine we're going to learn any more," Fran said.

We left the study and walked down the hall toward the front entry. Mildred stood near the closed sitting room door, silently guarding her mistress.

"Please tell Mrs. Dickson that we're leaving and thank her for her hospitality. If she needs anything, please ask her to call," Aunt Fran said, handing the maid her business card as we took our leave.

Mildred nodded and escorted us to the front door. The rain had stopped. Water droplets clung to shrubbery and a light steam rose off concrete surfaces heated by the summer sun. As we exited and headed toward our car, I spied Kevin Wyatt climb from his vehicle, parked on the street below. His face showed his surprise at seeing us as he scurried to reach the top of the drive before we could leave.

"What are you doing here?" Wyatt demanded between gasps for breath, winded after his run up the incline.

"Didn't your mama teach you any manners?" Fran asked as she faced the younger man. "Not that it's any of your business, but we've just paid a neighborly condolence call with Adele."

I faced the banker and met his stare. "We could ask the same. What are you doing here?"

"None of your business, although you tend to make it yours. By the way, you were seen the other night, you and your friend. Don't think because you're the wife of our sheriff that it gives you a free pass. I'm watching you, Mrs. Gardner."

I chose to stay silent and stared at him.

He turned in a huff and knocked loudly on the front door, ignoring the door chimes. We got into the car and drove away without a backward glance at the man. I wondered if it was true that we'd been seen at the meeting or if he was only tossing out some bait to see if I bit. I had to get with Colleen and find out what Ron told her about that vote.

Chapter Sixteen

Woodland Design

"You can drop me off at the store. I've still got some work to do before closing," Fran told me as I entered downtown and stopped before Frannie's Frocks.

"I'm going to talk with Colleen. I'll call you later," I said as she left the car.

"Okay. Let me know what you find online about that company name too."

"Will do." I waved goodbye then headed home.

The boys were still playing at Anna's house. I needed to take advantage of the quiet time while I had it and search my computer for any and all information on Woodland Design.

Mittens greeted me at the door as I tossed my purse onto the counter. He rubbed his back against my legs and purred loudly as I leaned down to pick him up. I cuddled my furry baby in my arms, petting his silky fur. He rewarded me with a head butt against my shoulder and a lick with his sandpaper tongue to my chin.

"Missed me, huh? Have you been a good boy today? Let's see what treats I can find in the cupboard," I told him as I entered the laundry room. Mittens wriggled out of my arms and dropped onto the floor next to his food dish. He was anything but subtle.

"Mrroww."

I filled his bowl with soft chicken-filled morsels which he loved and watched him dive into the treats with a contented purr as he chewed. Smiling at him, I pivoted and headed to my laptop waiting on the kitchen breakfast bar. First things first, I started a fresh pot of coffee to energize me while I searched the internet. Just smelling the fresh coffee grounds gave me a boost.

Opening up the search engine, I typed in the state of Ohio and brought up the Secretary of State page. If Woodland Design was a registered limited liability company, it should pop up by name on the business search page. My fingers tapped the keyboard and up sprung the newly formed LLC for Woodland Design with a registration date of October last year. Hmm, that was about the same time that rumors of the fracking started.

Pausing to pour a cup of the brewed coffee, I sipped the hot nectar thoughtfully as my mind raced to consider this new piece of information. I picked up my cell phone and punched in Colleen's number. She answered after the second ring.

"Hi Merry. Did you and Fran drop by Adele's today?"

"Yeah, we did. You should have seen that place ... huge mansion that puts Kirkland Manor to shame. Did you find out what the vote outcome was from Ron? Please tell me he told you and didn't hide behind that secret membership crap."

"He didn't want to tell me at first, but then I confessed to being there and after he got over that shock he admitted the vote was to disapprove the mining deal. Kevin Wyatt fumed and supposedly wanted to hold a second vote but all the members got up and left the building. That must have been what we saw when they all hurried out. So Ferguson is defeated. That's good news, right?"

"Yes, great news for Meadowood and the environment for sure.

Aunt Fran and I found a map that outlined the proposed property lease. You'll never guess where … right outside Granger's Farm and the Fox Run Park. Can you believe that? Mining so close to our town's recreation area. What a disaster that project would have been, if allowed to proceed with fracking close to town limits," I declared.

"Oh my goodness, no wonder there was such an uproar and opposition. Do you think Mayor Dickson would have approved that plan? I hate to think of him selling out his own town after being our mayor for so many years. Doesn't seem right."

"Well, you heard that guy in the S.O.F.M. meeting state that Dickson had changed his mind and it certainly seemed that way from Kevin Wyatt's anger. Maybe he would have vetoed the plan. Guess we'll never know but it may also have been a motive for someone to murder him … someone who was counting on making money with that deal. I'm trying to research the directors of a company called Woodland Design. That's who owns the land Ferguson intended to lease for his mining. If we could find who is really behind Woodland, we might learn who stood to gain by Dickson's death," I said.

The more I thought of the land deal, the more convinced I became. It made perfect sense as a motive for killing the person who objected to the deal. Money was always a factor, and this arrangement stood to make millions.

Eleven o'clock the next morning, Trixie Jones skipped into the tea shop with a grin that stretched from ear to ear. I waved her over to a table in the corner.

"Wait until you hear what John Ferguson had to say!" Trixie said in a loud whisper, her excitement bubbling over.

"I've got customers to wait on but I'm eager to hear. Can you wait? What can I bring you?"

"How about a cup of tea and some of those little tuna sandwiches you make? You're gonna burst when you hear my news," Trixie said.

"Be right back," I said as I hurried into the kitchen to plate three orders, Trixie's tuna, and poured cups of Earl Grey.

After serving three tables of customers, I hustled back to Trixie. I plopped onto a chair and waited between her bites of tuna to listen to her tale.

"So, Ferguson denied any lease negotiation with the city. But when I brought up Donald Dickson's death and implied that he might be a person of interest, well, you could see the steam come out of his ears! The man snapped a pencil in two that he was holding when I said that. I swear his face turned red. Sorry, I couldn't get any more because he had his security man throw me out of his office. It was so cool!" Trixie exclaimed, her face alight as she bounced on her chair.

"No doubt he is still licking his wounds because of the failed leasing deal. I know for a fact that the town council members and Meadowood's business community voted to deny the mining deal. Which is a positive thing. I'll give you the particulars later for your article."

"Great! I want to write about that fracking stuff and what dangers it poses. You said you knew where Ferguson intended to mine? How did you learn that?" Trixie asked.

"Let's just say that a map and the lease contract fell into my hands. The land in question is right outside Meadowood near the Fox Run Park and borders the former Granger farm. Both of those locations are prime recreational areas for our community. Can you imagine the disaster fracking would cause to that fragile environment?"

"Holy cow, this is a bigger story than just a murder. I can't thank you enough for bringing me in on this."

"Just write an honest and truthful account of all the facts. We're going to meet here later, after closing. Why don't you come back and join us."

"Yeah, okay. What else can I do for you?"

"Try to find out the names behind a company called Woodland Design. It's a limited liability company and I'd like to know the owners. The lease agreement included that name. Maybe your newspaper connections can uncover more than I could with an internet search."

"You got it."

Chapter Seventeen

Puzzle Pieces

The last customer had just left, and the small bell above the door tinkled softly as I flipped the "Open" sign to "Closed." The familiar scent of freshly brewed tea and warm pastries still lingered in the air, but the cozy atmosphere of the shop had taken on a more serious tone tonight. I glanced at the table where Aunt Fran, Anna, Colleen, and Trixie Jones gathered, their faces reflecting the same determined focus that was simmering in my own mind.

"Alright, ladies," I said, taking a deep breath and walking over to the whiteboard I'd set up in the shop's corner. "It's time we try to piece this puzzle together. If we're going to figure out what really happened to Donald Dickson, we need to look at everything we've got."

The whiteboard contained a few scattered comments, but tonight, I intended to get serious about organizing our thoughts. Erasing my previous notes, I uncapped a black marker and turned to the others. "Let's start with the clues we know."

Colleen leaned back in her chair, her arms crossed as she considered. "There's Fran's mayoral campaign button found near the body."

Aunt Fran sighed, her shoulders slumping a little. "I still can't believe it ... one of my buttons. I had my button pinned to my shirt,

Doug saw that. The campaign gave out hundreds during the parade. It could have belonged to anyone."

"I know, Aunt Fran," I said gently, turning to look at her. "But it was found right in the car. We have to consider it might be significant." I wrote *Campaign Button* on the board, underlining it for emphasis.

"Someone could've planted it there," Colleen interjected, her brow furrowed. "Maybe to throw suspicion off themselves and implicate Fran."

"Maybe it's a sign," Anna suggested, her brow furrowing. "Like someone was trying to send a message. Maybe whoever killed him wanted us to think it was politically motivated."

Trixie, who had been quietly observing, leaned forward. "Or it could be the opposite. Maybe it wasn't about politics at all, and the button was just a red herring. Something to throw us off the trail."

"That's possible," I agreed, jotting down a note beside the button. "We'll have to keep that in mind."

I tapped the marker against my chin, deep in thought. "Dickson had favored the lease with Ferguson and the property deal ... maybe he found out who owned Woodland Design and it changed his mind. And if the Society of Free Men was involved, it split his allegiance."

Trixie glanced at me sharply. "The Society? You think they're connected to all this? I heard whispers about some secret organization, but I didn't know it was real."

"It's a possibility," I said carefully, writing *S.O.F.M.* in bold letters at the top of the board. "We learned they've got their hands in a lot of things around here. If Donald was objecting to something that bene-fited their interests, they might have seen him as a problem that needed to be eliminated. The ironic thing is, even without Dickson's negative vote, Kevin Wyatt couldn't get enough yea's to pass the deal. They would have murdered Donald Dickson for nothing."

"Who owns Woodland Design?" Colleen asked.

"All I could find was the LLC registered with the state last year. It's a new company," I said as I added *Woodland Design* to our board.

Anna frowned. "Do we have any leads on that?"

Trixie shook her head. "Not yet. But I'm working on it. These things take time—LLCs are designed to protect the identities of the owners, so it's not easy to find out who's pulling the strings."

Colleen shivered slightly. "It's starting to sound like a conspiracy. But there's still one piece we haven't talked about—the mistress."

The room grew a little quieter at that, the weight of the word hanging in the air. Donald's unknown mistress had been a surprise discovery, one that none of us had expected. But it was a piece of the puzzle we couldn't ignore.

I added *Mistress* to the board, glancing around at the others. "This is the wild card. We know Donald was seeing someone on the side, but we don't know who. All we know about her comes from Margie at the diner. She's supposed to be young and not from Meadowood. If we could figure out her identity, it might tell us more about what was going on in his life—and who else might have had a motive to hurt him ... like his wife."

Aunt Fran sighed, folding her hands in her lap. "It's hard to imagine Donald being involved in something like that, but people are complicated. If this mistress was connected to any of the other pieces—Woodland Design, the Society—it could be a key to everything."

"We need to find out who she is," Anna said, her voice firm. "Do you honestly think a young girl is involved with this lease deal or a secret society of men? No, I think it's more basic than that. A crime of passion. Give me a woman scorned any day as the best motive," she said with a laugh.

Taking a red marker, I drew a map of the parade route and school grounds. Reconstructing the scene from memory, I drew small squares to represent cars and a long rectangle for the float truck. Next, I filled in small circles for the food vendors and picnic tents.

"I keep thinking of the *how* Dickson was murdered besides the *who*. How could the killer get close enough to harm him without being seen? Look at this." I tapped my marker on the board. "We all assembled in a precise order for the parade. Old Thelma Waverly rode in the front car as grand marshal, then behind her was the mayor's red Cadillac. Sheriff Simmons and Georgia followed in the Model-T, then the chamber float, and last, Colleen's car with Fran. The high school band and scouts marched behind all the vehicles with the fire trucks bringing up the rear."

"That's right. I got such a kick out of watching Missus Waverly. For someone one-hundred years old, she basked in all the attention as grand marshal," Anna remarked.

"Okay, so we know the mayor was seen waving to the crowds during the parade. He was uninjured at that point. When all the vehicles pulled into the lot next to the school, everyone just took whatever space was available. These squares are the cars. Does this look right, where everyone parked?"

I wrote a letter S on the square for Simmons, then marked a letter D for the car holding Dickson. The rectangle for the float parked next to Dickson's Cadillac. A letter C indicated Colleen's car parked two spaces over from the mayor, on the opposite side of Simmons.

"It was a tight fit. The chamber float took up a lot of room. I remember having to find a spot at the end of the line," Colleen added.

"By the time my scouts entered the area behind the band members, it was chaos and I couldn't even see the mayor's car. The tall float blocked it from view. In all the commotion, obviously someone took advantage of the moment. Aunt Fran, do you recall seeing anyone near the cars that wasn't part of the parade?"

"That's what Doug asked me. Honestly, I can't. After Colleen parked, I climbed out of the back and several women surrounded me with questions and well-wishes. There were so many people milling about, it took me several minutes to break free," Fran said as she pictured the scene in her mind.

"I'm sure Doug has a better timeline for all this, but I thought it might help us to sort of see the scene again. I was standing in line for food when I heard Georgia Simmons scream," I said.

"You know, if this drawing is supposed to account for everyone, it seems a bit off to me," Anna said as she stared at the board.

"What do you mean? I admit I'm not the best artist."

"There were food trucks arranged closer to the parking lot. They were spread out a bit more than what you're showing here. I remember thinking how far I had to walk to buy a funnel cake for Stevie and wished he'd wanted a snow cone instead because that truck sat closer," Anna said.

"Interesting." I erased my circle icons and spread them across the map, allowing more space to show their locations. "Like this?" I asked.

"Yeah, I think so. I don't remember which food vendor occupied each spot, but I think the snow cones were in this one because there was a trail of water running down the pavement from under his truck. I recall skirting it so my feet didn't get wet," Anna said in memory as she pointed to the vendor circle I had drawn closest to the parked vehicles.

I turned back to the board, looking at the collection of clues we'd gathered. The campaign button, the mining lease, the property owned by Woodland Design, the mysterious mistress, and the shadowy presence of the Society of Free Men—all of it connected, somehow. We just had to figure out how.

Chapter Eighteen

Three Strikes You're Out

Eight days had passed since Meadowood's Bicentennial parade and Donald Dickson's death. The final day of the community celebration found us at the ball park. Meadowood Lions faced the Pottstown Tigers in a quest for little league baseball championship and fame. Doug and I climbed the bleacher seats to the top row, where we could view the game and our son Johnny in his shortstop position. Billy insisted on standing at the fence behind home plate to cheer his brother on.

Everyone in town was at the big game. I spied Kevin Wyatt with a group of men standing near the fence. As I watched him, his head pivoted to me, like radar, and glared his hatred. I nudged Doug and pointed to the banker, but the man quickly melted into the crush.

Seats filled up rapidly as the home town population poured in. Meadowood had won the coin toss to host the game, making Pottstown the visitors. Tiger fans occupied the smaller stands to our left between home plate and third base. Our home stands were erected behind home plate and toward first base, with a narrow opening between the two structures. The fans cheered as the teams strode onto the field and headed toward their individual dugouts.

I waved to Anna and Chuck as they found seats in the third row far below us. Anna wasn't big on climbing into the nose bleed higher seats. They were so proud of their son, Stevie, playing the key position of team pitcher. That boy had a really strong arm and a fast ball that could make professional ball players envious. When future scouts get a load of his pitching, he'll be sure to win a scholarship to whatever college he chooses.

Now we had to wait until the national anthem played and the umpire called "play ball" for the game to begin. I leaned in to Doug's shoulder, mostly so he could hear me over the crowd's noise and also so no one else would listen to my words.

"How's the case going? Are you close to making an arrest?"

"You know I can't talk to you about that. But I'll be honest with you. This case is frustrating. All my suspects have solid alibis and I'm coming up empty on my search for someone new. I know there's a missing link; I just haven't found it yet."

"Did you find the woman in Pottstown that he was seeing? My sources swear he cheated on Adele. Kind of gives her a good motive to kill him. Isn't it always the spouse who's the prime suspect?"

A shout from the crowd and the blaring of trumpets interrupted his reply as the band responded with its version of the national anthem. We all stood and placed our right hands over our hearts.

Talking became impossible during the game. Too much fanfare, music, and riotous cheers to hear anything. During the bottom of the seventh inning, nature called. I tapped Doug on the arm and pantomimed that I was leaving for the restroom. He nodded as I carefully made my way down the high bleacher steps then finally gained solid ground.

It was slow going through throngs of people as I headed toward the concession stand and the attached rest rooms. I noticed a group of food trucks parked nearby supplemented the standard hot dog concession menu. Mentally promising myself a funnel cake or perhaps a snow cone, I entered the building then waited in line for the bathroom with other women who all had the same idea. Or maybe we mothers were just at a similar age and our bladders ruled. Why is it the men's room never had a line? Didn't seem fair.

After finally taking care of my needs, I wandered toward the food trucks to determine what other treats tempted hungry fans. One entrepreneur sold slices of hot pizza and another hawked the usual sweet treats of spun cotton candy, caramel popcorn, and funnel cakes. As I walked past the snow cone truck, I stared at the vendor scraping a block of ice. He looked familiar to me. Raising his head, his hand paused in his task and his eyes met mine. He frowned. I tried to place him; I'd seen him somewhere but couldn't put my finger on it. A chill went through me that had nothing to do with the frozen ice treats.

I turned away and hurried back to the truck selling funnel cakes.

"One please," I said as I pulled my wallet from my pocket and counted out three dollars for the cake. "Thank you."

It smelled heavenly. I couldn't wait to devour a piece. Funnel cakes always brought out the kid in me. By the time I got back to my seat, I was sure I'd be wearing a dusting of powdered sugar ... the peril of eating the deliciously sweet cake. I paused next to the last food truck before heading to the stands. Concentrating on balancing the funnel cake on its flimsy paper plate, I broke off a small piece. Just as I placed the cake into my mouth, I felt a thump on the back of my head. My knees buckled and I dropped to the ground; the funnel cake slid out of my outstretched hand. I saw a pair of work boots standing next to me before my eyes closed and my world turned black.

"Merry! Come on honey, wake up. Merry, can you hear me?"

Doug's voice sounded so far away. I felt a gentle hand caress my face. My eyes fluttered; I tried to focus. Why did my head spin? It hurt to move. The desire to close my eyes and go back to sleep was over-whelming.

An insistent hand kept shaking my shoulder. I heard other voices. My body was lifted. I felt a soft surface then a blanket cuddled me. I opened my eyes to recognize my husband's worried face as he held my hand and walked next to a pair of paramedics. They slid me into the back of an ambulance and Doug climbed in next to me.

"What happened?" I asked in a whisper, my throat dry and hoarse.

"You've got a head injury. Do you remember anything? Did you fall?" Doug asked.

"What? No ... I bought a funnel cake ... then. I think someone hit me."

Doug's expression reflected his concern then anger at my words. After fifteen years of marriage, I could read him pretty well despite how he tried to present a blank look. His hand squeezed mine tighter and I knew I had read him correctly.

"When you didn't come back right away, I got worried and went to look for you. I searched the bathroom and food trucks. Then a woman yelled for help. When I ran toward her, she pointed behind the building. I found you laying on the ground partially hidden by a dumpster behind the concession building."

"Eww, that's why I smell like garbage. I just want a shower and an aspirin in that order."

"You're going to the hospital and get checked out. You've got a goose egg on the back of your head and were unconscious. The doctor will tell you when it's safe for you to come home," he insisted.

"What about the boys? Are they okay? Who won the game?" I asked as my thoughts suddenly flew to my sons and I tried to get up.

"Whoa! You lie still. Johnny and Billy are going home with Anna. They're okay, don't worry about them. The Lions won. Stevie pitched a shutout in the ninth inning that clinched the win 7-6. Now close your eyes and rest."

"All right. You don't have to be such a bully. Um, Doug ... maybe I should tell you that Kevin Wyatt threatened me when I ran into him at Adele Dickson's house the other day.

I saw him at the game and he kinda gave me one of those *if looks could kill* expressions."

"Why would Wyatt threaten you?"

"He might have seen me at the S.O.F.M. meeting," I said in a soft voice as I drifted back to sleep.

Doug stared at his sleeping wife. He shook his head. Of course, she attended a secret men's meeting. Why would he think otherwise? Merry had a habit of poking her nose into places where she had no business. But that didn't give Kevin Wyatt the right to threaten or harm her. Wyatt had some explaining to do. Doug planned on hauling him into the station as soon as Meredith's condition became stable and it was safe to leave her.

Don't let anyone tell you that hospitals are restful. Far from it. After undergoing a series of scans and tests then being pinched and prodded, doctors finally released me later that night. I was truly looking forward to some sleep in my own bed.

Even that delightful thought had to wait. A half hour after walking through the door, Aunt Fran and Colleen rushed over with Anna and Trixie close on their heels. Anna instantly took command of my kitchen and brewed a pot of tea then served a plate of cookies, compliments of Martha's bakery. Everyone grouped around me, asking a dozen questions at once as I reclined on the sofa. I couldn't really complain about the outpouring of love from my dear friends and family. Having people care for you was a nice feeling.

"You scared us half to death," Anna drawled as she poured me a cup of tea.

"Does Doug know who did this?" asked my aunt.

"Do you think this has anything to do with our snooping?" Colleen asked, frown lines wrinkling her pretty brow.

I held up my hand to stop their questions; their voices blending as one as they each tried to speak.

"Please, you're giving me a headache. All I can recall is going to the ladies room then walking past the food trucks and buying a funnel cake. I didn't even get a bite of it when I felt a thump and fell to the ground. I guess whoever hit me must have dragged me behind the concession building. I'll have to burn my clothes, they stink so bad from the garbage I laid in."

"How horrible!" Aunt Fran said as she patted my arm. "I'm just glad you weren't seriously injured."

"I saw Kevin Wyatt while I was sitting in the stands. Man, he gave me such a nasty look. I wouldn't put it past him to be the one that clobbered me. Remember what he said, Aunt Fran, when we were leaving Adele's house? The man practically threatened me."

"Did you ever tell Doug about his threats? Does he know we were at that society meeting?" Colleen asked.

"Yeah, I told him about Wyatt's threats and had to confess we were inside the meeting. I didn't go into details and I think he'd prefer not knowing to keep his sanity," I said with a laugh. I held the top of my head; it throbbed with my erratic movement. "Oh oww, it hurts to laugh."

"You better take it easy for the next day or so. I can handle the tea shop. No need for you to come in," Anna stated.

"Oh hey, I'll give you a hand. I don't know how to make those fancy sandwiches you guys serve, but I can carry a tray of cups and serve folks," Trixie offered.

"That's very kind of you. Thank you," I said and smiled at the young gal. She was proving my first impressions of her wrong and I had to admit to a growing fondness for Trixie.

"I've got a bit of news that might help you feel better," Trixie said.

We all turned our attention to her. She beamed as she announced her findings.

"Guess who the owners are of the Woodland Design LLC? Give up?

Would you believe none other than Kevin Wyatt and Adele Hayes, aka Adele Dickson?"

You could have heard a pin drop in the dead silence her words created. The shock ended. We all gasped as one.

"Wow, I didn't see that one coming," I said.

"Hmm, seems Kevin might have had a different reason for visiting the widow than just condolence," Aunt Fran speculated.

"Certainly shines a new light on who stood to gain by that leasing deal and why Donald Dickson may have been killed," Anna voiced all our thoughts.

"I've got to share this information with Doug. It might be the clue he was looking for to break this case open. Are you certain about your facts? Do you have any written evidence?"

"Yep, sure do. I reached out to my cousin that works in Columbus at the state office building. She's friends with a guy in the commerce department. Anyway, she managed to look up the registration of that company and made a copy of the original filing, complete with signatures."

Smiling at her enthusiasm, I had to admit she had accomplished what I couldn't in finding the owner's names.

Trixie reached into her purse and pulled out a folded paper then handed it to me. No doubt about it ... Kevin and Adele were in business together. What else were they entangled in?

Chapter Nineteen

Wyatt

"Betty's running the shop. I had to come over this morning and see for myself how you were feeling. Did you get any rest?" Fran scurried about the kitchen, loading the kid's dirty dishes into the dishwasher and fixing me a scrambled egg and toast for breakfast. She carried the food plus a steaming cup of coffee on a tray and set it down before me as I reclined against a pile of pillows on the sofa.

"You don't have to do that. I could have gone into the kitchen to eat. I'm not an invalid. Admittedly, the room spun a bit when I tried to stand earlier so I thought I'd just lay here a minute. But really, I'm fine."

"Mm-hmm. Head injuries are nothing to sneeze at. You need to rest and heal. Take today to relax. Nothing is more important than your health. This penchant for snooping into police matters has to stop," Fran said, a worried expression on her face as she directed me to eat then poured herself a coffee.

I chose to ignore her mother hen's comments. "You know, I've been thinking about what Trixie told us and our visit to Adele's house. Don't you think it's odd that she allowed us access to Donald's study, knowing we'd see a copy of the lease agreement?" I asked between bites of the delicious food. I was hungrier than I thought.

"Perhaps she felt protected by the LLC, her identity hidden. I don't think anyone would suspect her to being a party to Woodland Design. Basically Adele was hiding in plain sight and no doubt thought we weren't smart enough to see it," Fran said. She sipped her coffee and petted Mittens, who had joined her on her lap.

"Do you think that's it? Adele pretended to be ignorant of the lease deal because her name wasn't on any paperwork."

"It gave her plausible deniability unless someone delved into the ownership of that company. I'm sure she never dreamt her involvement would become known."

"So what do we do now?" I asked.

"Maybe it's time for Trixie to publish her exposé and watch the fallout when everyone in Meadowood reads the facts."

"Wow, that's going to shake the town's timbers."

Sheriff Douglas Gardner stood in the sheriff's office, his eyes locked on the man seated across from him. Kevin Wyatt, one of Meadowood's two prominent bankers, sat with an air of practiced ease, his polished demeanor at odds with the tension filling the room. The office was simple—paneled walls, a single window looking out onto the quiet main street, and a large oak desk between Doug and Wyatt. Deputy Tony Dalton stood near the door, his arms crossed, watching the exchange with the same intensity as Doug.

Kevin Wyatt was a handsome man, well-dressed in a tailored suit that seemed out of place in the small town, but perfectly in line with his cultivated image. His dark hair was neatly combed, and his expensive watch gleamed in the low light of the room. He met Doug's gaze with a confident smile that barely reached his eyes, betraying none of the anxiety Doug had hoped to see.

"So," Doug began, his voice low and steady, though the anger simmering beneath the surface was palpable, "you were at the little league game. People saw you there. Funny thing, my wife was there too. And now, she's lying at home with a concussion. You wouldn't happen to know anything about that, would you?"

Wyatt's smile widened, and he leaned back in his chair, crossing one leg over the other. "Sheriff, I'm as concerned as anyone about what happened to Merry. But to imply I had something to do with it? That's quite a leap, don't you think?"

Doug's jaw tightened. He'd like to wipe that smug smile off his face. He leaned forward, resting his hands on the desk between them. "Is it? You threatened her, Wyatt. She was looking into your dealings with Dickson and that fracking lease, and you didn't like it one bit. You told her to stay out of it. And now, after she poked around again, she winds up hurt."

Wyatt sighed, as if dealing with a particularly troublesome client. "I'll admit, I wasn't thrilled about Merry's interest in the Society's affairs. But I'm a businessman, Sheriff. I don't go around attacking people, especially not your wife. Is it my fault you can't control your wife's meddling? If anything, I've tried to keep her safe from getting mixed up in things she doesn't understand."

Doug's fists clenched at his sides. "Watch it, Wyatt. You call threatening Merry, keeping her safe?

"Sometimes, a warning is all it takes," Wyatt replied coolly. "But I didn't lay a hand on her. I wouldn't."

Tony stepped forward, his voice firm but measured. "Kevin, this isn't just about you being at the game. It's about you being involved in something that goes deeper than a little league match. Our office is investigating the mayor's murder, and your name keeps coming up—alongside Adele Dickson's. You want to explain your relationship with the widow?"

Wyatt's expression hardened slightly at the mention of Adele, but he maintained his calm exterior. "Adele and I are business associates, that's all. The Ferguson mining deal was above board, Sheriff. The Society voted not to pursue it. It had nothing to do with Dickson's death, and certainly nothing to do with what happened to Merry."

Doug's eyes narrowed, his voice taking on a dangerous edge. "You think I'm stupid, Wyatt? You think I don't know what you are really up to? That land deal wasn't just about money—it was about power. Dickson opposed it, and now he's dead. Where were you after the bicentennial parade ended? I hope you have a solid alibi. Merry found out about your deal with Ferguson Mining, and you didn't like it. Her reporter friend was ready to expose you and your reckless plan for Meadowood. You had motive for both Dickson's murder and Merry's assault."

Wyatt's smile faded, and for the first time, a flicker of irritation crossed his face. "Doug, I understand you're upset. Merry is your wife, and you want to protect her. But you're letting your emotions cloud your judgment. I had nothing to do with the mayor's death or what happened to Merry. I wasn't even near the concession stand where she was found. You're barking up the wrong tree."

Doug's voice dropped to a low growl. "You know, Wyatt, I've seen a lot of men try to talk their way out of trouble in this room. But you—you're something else. You think you're untouchable because you've got money, connections. But let me tell you something. In Meadowood, we don't care about any of that. We care about what's right. I will learn about your involvement with Dickson's death. And if you hurt Merry too, I will find out. And when I do, no amount of smooth talking or fancy suits will save you."

Wyatt leaned forward, his eyes narrowing as he matched Doug's intensity. "I'm not the enemy here, Doug. I didn't hurt Merry. If you want to find out who did, maybe you should start looking at the people who have the most to gain from her being out of the picture. She ruffles a lot of feathers. There are many folks in this town who don't want the truth about Dickson's business or his extra-marital affairs come to light. But I'm not one of them."

Doug stood up, the chair scraping loudly against the wooden floor as he did. His voice was steady, but the fury was evident in every word. "You're lying. I can see it. I can hear it in your voice. And I'm going to prove it."

Wyatt stood as well, meeting Doug's glare with a calm that only infuriated the sheriff more. "You're wrong, Sheriff. But if you're so sure of yourself, then by all means, continue your investigation. I've got nothing to hide."

Doug took a step closer, his voice a low hiss. "You should start praying I don't find out you're involved, Wyatt. Because if I do, I'll make sure you pay for what you've done."

Tony, sensing the rising tension, stepped between them, placing a hand on Doug's shoulder.

"All right Wyatt. Get out of here. You're free to go ... for the time being," Tony said.

Wyatt straightened his suit jacket, smoothing the fabric as if the entire exchange had been a minor inconvenience.

"This isn't over, Wyatt," Doug said, his voice steady but filled with promise. "Not by a long shot."

"I wouldn't expect it to be, Sheriff. But I suggest you focus your efforts where they'll do the most good."

He stepped out of the office and closed the door on the two lawmen. Wyatt allowed himself a small, satisfied smile. He had weathered the storm, but he knew it wasn't the last he'd seen of Sheriff Douglas Gardner. The game was far from over, and Wyatt was more than ready to play.

"Doug, you always told me we need to keep a clear head. Wyatt's not going anywhere. We'll keep digging, and we'll find out the truth."

Doug nodded slightly. He had allowed his personal emotions to get the better of him. Tony knew it, and so did Wyatt. It was unprofessional. This case had him frustrated to the point he wasn't thinking straight. Time to correct that.

Stepping outside, Doug paused on the steps of the sheriff's office, staring out into the peaceful town of Meadowood. The sun was setting, casting long shadows across the street. He clenched his fists, taking a deep breath to calm the rage that still boiled within him.

"Tony," he said finally, his voice low, "I want round-the-clock surveillance on Kevin Wyatt. If he so much as sneezes, I want to know about it."

Tony nodded. "You got it, Sheriff. We'll keep a close watch."

Doug nodded, his eyes still fixed on the horizon. "He's hiding something. I know it. And I'm going to find out what it is."

Tony placed a reassuring hand on Doug's shoulder. "We'll get to the bottom of this. Together."

As they stood there, the last rays of sunlight disappearing behind the hills, Doug knew one thing for certain: the battle for the truth was just beginning. He wouldn't rest until he caught Donald Dickson's murderer and found whoever had injured his wife. Justice must be served. If that net captured Kevin Wyatt too, so much the better.

Chapter Twenty

Exposed

My phone rang in that insistent ring tone that usually spelled bad news. Finally, I silenced the noise by grabbing the receiver as I shot a look at the clock ... six-thirty. This had better be good.

"Hello?" I mumbled as I rubbed sleep out of my eyes.

"Did I wake you?" Anna asked.

"Of course you did. Why are you awake so early? What's wrong?" My attention focused, and I threw back the covers as my feet hit the floor. I could hear water running in the bathroom as Doug shaved and dressed for work.

"Guess you haven't seen the newspaper yet. Trixie's story is plastered across the front page. Oh my God, wait until you read it. You know what is gonna hit the fan!"

"Let me get dressed and grab a cup of coffee to get awake. I'll call you back," I told her then stumbled into the bathroom.

A quick shower and twenty minutes later, I sipped hot coffee as I read the Tribune retrieved from my doorstep. Anna was right when she said the story was plastered across the front page, complete with photos of the main characters: Donald and Adele Dickson, Kevin Wyatt, and a blank silhouette of the mystery mistress. Holy cow! Trixie spun a story that made Meadowood sound like a cross between *Peyton Place* and *Dynasty*. It gave the town gossips enough fodder to chew on for a year.

I read the article a second time. Trixie spelled out the proposed deal between Ferguson Mining and Woodland Design to lease a parcel of land that bordered one of Meadowood's recreational areas. She explained the dangers of fracking and the pollution to the land and water. Next, Trixie outlined the revenue to be gained by the owners of that land and then listed their names. It would be a shocking revelation to the townsfolk to see Adele Hayes Dickson and Kevin Wyatt partners in the plot to ravage our community.

Trixie divulged the secrets of the Society of Free Men and its role in the mining lease agreement; how a group of Meadowood businessmen sought to control the lives of the entire town and its well-being. I could only guess at the surprise and feminine outrage the women in our town must be feeling when they read that news.

She continued her article speculating on the motives behind the murder of Mayor Donald Dickson. Was it a love triangle? Did his wife plot to murder him because he objected to her get-rich plans? Readers would naturally jump to the conclusion that Kevin Wyatt and Adele Dickson were in a romantic affair. But what of Donald's gossiped cheating? Trixie described the young woman in question as a resident of Pottstown but didn't list her name. Her identity was either not known or was being protected by the Tribune. No matter which, the ladies of Meadowood and the gossips of Pottstown would be wagging tongues as they hung over fence tops and burned up the telephone lines comparing notes. Speculation on the young woman would be rife.

I heard a quick tap on my back door then Colleen rushed into the kitchen. She clutched the newspaper in one hand as she expressively waved with the other.

"Did you read it? Oh my gosh! Everyone I know has their nose in the paper," Colleen said breathlessly, her face flushed. She helped herself to a cup of coffee and one of the bran muffins I had baked earlier as she took a seat at the counter.

"Mm-hmm. Anna woke me at dawn screaming about the article. I've read it twice. Trixie did a thorough job covering all the facts and the players involved. Don't you think? I bet Kevin Wyatt must be ready to spit nails. I wonder if his position at the bank is in jeopardy. Can you just imagine what the gossip level must be down at the Cut & Curl this morning?" I snorted as an image sprung to my mind.

"Well, Trixie painted Adele Dickson in an unflattering light. She practically accused her of either killing Donald or plotting against him with Wyatt against the entire town. Either way, I doubt Meadowood folks will look kindly toward her. She might as well start packing now."

"Did you notice the tiny blurb on page six of the Tribune about the Republican party replacement for mayoral candidate? It says Louis Harper, from the town council, has been chosen to assume Dickson's spot on the ticket. Looks like Aunt Fran has an opposing candidate after all. As her campaign manager, what are your plans before election day? Will you do another debate?" I asked.

Colleen put her half-eaten muffin on a napkin and hastily flipped through the newspaper until she located the brief article about Harper. Her eyebrow raised as she read the notice.

"Hmm, that's the first I heard about Harper jumping into the race. There's no time for another debate. The election is in two days. I need to get Fran out and about though, talking to folks and pushing her case for mayor, especially now that she has an opponent."

"Speak of the devil, here she is now," I said as my aunt strode into the kitchen. "Were your ears burning? Colleen just said she had to talk to you."

"No, what about? Did you see where Louis Harper plans to run against me? I almost missed the notice in today's paper. Is it legal? Does he have enough time to submit his name on the ballot before the election?" Fran asked as she also took a seat and grabbed a muffin with her coffee.

"That's what we were just discussing. Yes, under these emergency circumstances, filing deadline was last night by midnight. He had to have filed with the board of elections yesterday or the newspaper wouldn't have had the information to publish. So I guess he filed in time," Colleen answered. "Can you have Betty run the shop today so you can do some door to door visiting and old-fashioned handshaking? We need to get you out among the voters and remind them who will make the best mayor."

"Sure, I can do that. Let's start about eleven. That gives me time to open the shop and fill in Betty about my plans. I'll still have plenty of time to walk the neighborhood. Hopefully, we can make the rounds before that predicted rain storm hits. Where do you want to start?" Fran asked.

"Let me plot some streets. I'll have a route by the time I meet you at eleven," Colleen answered as she began making notes on her phone.

As I placed my cup and breakfast plate in the dishwasher, Anna rushed through the door. A blast of chilly air swept in with her. She took in the scene then let out a deep breath.

"Good! Everyone is here, except Trixie, but she's probably busy at the Tribune. Her story is all anyone can talk about this morning. My phone has been ringing off the hook," Anna said.

"Yep, I think everyone in the county has read that article. It certainly made an impression. The tea shop will be buzzing when we open today. Speaking of which ... we better get in gear."

"Do you think it will be safe? I keep thinking of Kevin Wyatt and his anger about being investigated. Will he make trouble for us? Did Doug accuse him of hitting you over the head? I saw him at the bank so I know he's not under arrest," Anna said.

"No arrest but Doug assured me he's got him under constant surveillance. We'll be okay. Trixie didn't state who her sources were and no one except Wyatt knows that Colleen and I attended the Society meeting. Of course, Adele is aware of Fran and me searching Donald's files, but then she gave us her permission. If anyone might hold a grudge, it could be Adele," I said. I took care of the other dirty coffee mugs and swiped a dishtowel across the counter surface.

Dickson's murder and the subsequent scandals in town were on all our minds as we headed out, each woman ready to face the day and the next crisis.

Chapter Twenty-One

Revenge

Leaves flew by and wind rattled the windows as Anna and I sipped our tea, our usual late afternoon ritual after closing. We'd been busier than usual and as we had predicted, the topic on everyone's lips was the scandalous article in the Tribune. Speculation ran high on motives for Dickson's death and the shock of learning he'd had a mistress. We found ourselves finally alone.

The empty tea shop was unusually quiet, almost too quiet, considering the storm brewing outside. The heavy clouds mirrored the unease in my stomach. I couldn't put my finger on the impression of impending danger that I felt.

I glanced at Anna, noticing the way her hands trembled slightly as she reached for her cup. She tried to hide it, but I could see the anxiety in her eyes. This sudden storm and the tension in town since the news article released had us all on edge. I opened my mouth to say something reassuring when the door violently swung open, the bell clanging out in protest. I had forgotten to lock it after flipping the sign to closed.

A tall gaunt figure, framed by the gloom outside, stood in the doorway. His eyes, sharp and cold, locked onto me with a predatory intensity that sent a chill down my spine. He didn't belong in my tea shop, not in this cozy, safe haven I had created. But here he was, and there was no mistaking the desperation in his face.

"Merry Gardner," he said, his voice low and menacing, "I knew you'd be here."

"Do I know you? Who are you?" I replied evenly, setting down my cup. I stared at his face. "I've seen you before. What do you want?"

"My name's Silas Conner. You and your friends have made my poor daughter's life a living hell. She can't step out of the house, afraid to show her face with the shame you brought down on her."

"I'm afraid I don't understand. Who is your daughter? What makes you think I'd want to harm her?" I asked in a level tone. I slipped my cell phone out of my apron pocket and under the cover of the hanging tablecloth, I dialed Doug's number at the sheriff's office.

"That newspaper article. I saw you talking with that reporter, filling her head with lies about my girl … casting my poor Molly as a wanton woman. That ain't true. She's a good girl and Donald Dickson took advantage of her with his empty promises. He deserved to die for what he did to my sweet girl." Silas paced the floor and looked anxiously out the window as the rain pelted the glass. The overhead lights glinted off the wicked knife blade held by his side.

Anna's eyes widened, and I could feel the tension in the room ratchet up several notches. She was scared, and I couldn't blame her.

Silas was a dangerous man—more dangerous than I could have imagined.

"You know why I'm here," he snarled, stepping further into the shop. "You've been snooping around, asking questions, following me. I can't allow that."

I kept my voice calm, steady. "I wasn't following you. Your daughter's name wasn't even in the paper. I was only trying to find out the truth, Silas. About what happened to Mayor Dickson."

Silas laughed, but there was no humor in it, only bitterness. "The truth is that man ruined my daughter's life. He promised her everything and left her with nothing but a scandal that destroyed us all." His pacing stopped by the door as he clicked the lock on the handle and lowered the window blind.

Anna shifted beside me, trying to make herself smaller. I could see her eyes darting to the exit, but there was no way out. Not now. Not with Silas blocking the door.

"You didn't have to kill him, Silas," I whispered, trying to reach the part of him that might still be rational. "There were other ways. The election would have voted him out of office. His wife was ready to leave him; he'd have been a broken man ... a failure, if you'd left him alone."

His face contorted in rage. "No. You don't know what it was like, watching her suffer, watching our lives fall apart because of his lies. But I took care of him. I saw my chance at the end of the parade. Nobody noticed me in the crowd with my ice pick. It was easy."

Ice pick ... now I recalled where I'd seen him. Silas sold the snow cones at the parade and at the ball field. It made sense now, the drops of water on the car seat from a wet ice pick. The girl crying at the funeral— Molly was there with her father.

My hand slipped under the tablecloth, fingers brushing against the smooth surface of my cell phone. I hoped Doug was listening. I just had to keep Silas talking until he got here.

"I understand you're angry," I said, forcing myself to hold his gaze. "But this isn't the answer. Hurting more people won't provide your daughter a better future. Revenge is never the answer."

"She's all I have left," he whispered, and for a moment, I saw the anguish in his eyes. But it was gone as quickly as it appeared, replaced by a wild desperation. "And you ... you've seen too much. I couldn't risk you connecting the dots, so I had to stop you at the ballgame."

Anna gasped softly beside me. "You ... you're the one who hit Merry?"

Silas nodded, his expression grim. "I didn't want to, but you left me no choice. You stared at me and I thought you recognized me from the funeral or from the parade."

"What about the campaign button, Silas? Was that yours? Why did you leave it in the car?" My curiosity won out over my fear. I had to know.

"Yeah, I was wearing it; some girl gave it to me. Guess it got snagged on the seatbelt harness and fell off when I reached across to stab him. I didn't have time to pick it up."

I could hear the faint sound of the back door creaking. We never found time to oil those hinges. It had to be Doug finding a way inside. But I couldn't let my relief show, not yet.

"Silas, this will not end well for you," I said, trying to keep him focused on me. "You need to stop now, before it's too late."

He hesitated, the conflict clear on his face, as he stepped toward us. And then, in a blur of motion, Doug was there, moving swiftly and silently. He grabbed Silas from behind, pulling him away from me and Anna, pinning his arms behind his back.

"It's over, Silas," Doug said firmly, his voice a steady anchor in the chaos.

Silas struggled for a moment, but it was futile. The fight went out of him all at once, leaving him a hollow, broken man. Doug secured him quickly, then turned to me, concern etched on his face.

"Are you okay?" he asked, his eyes scanning me for injuries.

I nodded, though my heart was still racing. "I'm fine, thanks to you."

Anna finally exhaled, the tension draining from her in a rush. "That was too close," she whispered, her voice shaky.

Doug led Silas toward the door, but the man stopped and looked back at me, his eyes filled with a sorrow that was almost unbearable to see. "I just wanted justice for her," he sobbed.

"I know," I replied, my voice barely above a whisper.

As Doug guided him out into the waiting storm, I couldn't shake the feeling that, in his own twisted way, Silas had been trying to do the right thing. But it was too late for him, and too late for the peace he sought.

Anna reached out and took my hand, her grip warm and reassuring. "You were so brave," she said, her voice filled with admiration.

I managed a small smile, but inside, I felt anything but brave. The confrontation had been too close, too real. Meadowood proved to be no better or no worse than other small towns. Its citizens all held secrets: private and personal, but some dark and menacing that when left to run rampant had the power to tear the town apart.

Chapter Twenty-Two

Election

Polls closed. Workers tallied ballots. In the final outcome, Louis Harper hadn't stood a chance against Frances Andrews in the mayoral race. Time to welcome a new administration.

The air was thick with the final days of summer. The scent of freshly cut grass mingled with the aroma of grilled food. A string of twinkling lights stretched across the yard, illuminating the happy faces of family and friends, their laughter filling the warm evening air. Aunt Fran's election victory was cause for celebration, and there was no better place than my own backyard to toast to the future of Meadowood.

I wiped my hands on a dish towel and stepped out onto the deck, where I could see everyone gathered. Colleen and Ron chatted with Anna and Chuck near the buffet table, while neighbors and friends Teresa, Martha, and Carol all shared an animated conversation by the flowerbeds. Ted and Barb Williams were standing next to Betty admiring the banner we had strung up, which read, "Congratulations, Mayor Andrews!"

The banner wasn't the only thing catching attention. Aunt Fran stood at the center of the gathering, her face glowing with pride, flanked by her supporters. She had worked tirelessly to win this election, and it showed. After everything Meadowood had been through—the scandal, the murder of Mayor Dickson, and the mining deal that nearly ruined us all—it felt good to breathe easy again.

I walked over to Fran, catching snippets of conversation as I passed through the crowd.

"I can't believe it's finally over," Carol was saying, shaking her head. "That mess with the mining company had us all on edge."

Martha nodded. "Thank goodness the truth behind the mining deal was uncovered. We would've had fracking right next to the park if it weren't for Merry and that reporter Trixie Jones digging into things."

"Who would have thought Donald Dickson would meet his maker at the hands of a disgruntled father. I kind of feel sorry for Silas Conner. He was only defending his daughter Molly. Three cheers to our brave sheriff, Doug Gardner, for capturing the killer and preventing any more injuries," Teresa toasted as she held her glass high.

"Guess the arrest of a killer and closing the case should put to rest any doubts about our new sheriff," Trixie stated as she toasted to one and all.

"Our new sheriff? Did I hear that right? Are you residing in Meadowood now?" I asked Trixie as I gave her a quick hug.

"Yep. Feels like a nice place to live, even if it has some quirky residents. Besides, where else could I find the perfect cup of tea?" Trixie said with a laugh.

"Welcome to the neighborhood," Anna told Trixie, overhearing our conversation.

I smiled to myself, rather proud of my part in saving my community. The end to the leasing deal between Ferguson Mining and the Woodland Design company stopped the fracking plan dead in its tracks. I was even prouder of my handsome husband for saving the day, plus Anna and me from harm, when he surprised Silas Conner in our tea shop.

Meadowood was safe, for now.

As I reached Fran, she turned to me with that warm smile of hers.

"Merry, darling, this party is absolutely wonderful! You've outdone yourself."

"Well, you deserve it, Aunt Fran," I said, giving her a hug. "This is your night."

Fran's eyes sparkled. "You know, I never imagined I'd be standing here as mayor. But it feels right. Like this town is ready for something new."

Before I could respond, Colleen and Ron approached with glasses of champagne. "To the new mayor!" Colleen said, raising her glass.

"To Fran!" we all echoed, clinking glasses. The bubbles tickled my nose, and I couldn't help but feel a surge of pride for my aunt.

"Now that we're all toasting, Aunt Fran, do you want to tell everyone about your first big decision?" I teased, knowing full well she had something up her sleeve.

Fran grinned, setting down her glass. "Oh, I've been waiting to make this announcement all night. I've decided that my first act as mayor will be to officially dissolve the Society of Free Men."

A murmur ran through the crowd, but it was more of a collective agreement than surprise. A secret fraternal organization pulling strings behind the political scenes was heartily voted down by the majority of the town's population.

"Good riddance to them," mumbled Martha Parker, owner of the bakery Martha's Delites. The female business owners in town had voiced their ire at the discovery of an exclusively male organization that proposed itself as the town's leaders with their omission.

Fran held up her hand. "Not only will the Society be no more, but all of their historic artifacts—yes, even the ones they tried to hide—will reside in our new Meadowood history museum for everyone to see. We'll respect their colonial history as just that, but no more secrets. And from now on, local government is going to be for everyone, not just a select few."

"Madam Mayor, may I quote you on that?" asked Trixie.

The cheers that erupted were deafening. I saw Ted Williams clapping his hands together, his face beaming with approval. Even Betty, Fran's sales clerk at the dress shop, who usually kept to herself, was smiling and nodding in agreement.

"I'll drink to that," Barb said, lifting her glass.

I caught Fran's eye, and we exchanged a look. We both knew this wasn't just about getting rid of some old secret society. It was about moving Meadowood forward, making sure everyone had a voice in our town's future.

As the crowd dispersed into smaller groups, I found myself standing next to Anna, who had Chuck's arm looped through hers. She leaned in and whispered, "Did you see Adele Dickson today? She put a 'For Sale' sign in her yard."

I nodded. "I did. Can't say I'm surprised. After everything that happened with the mining scandal and Kevin Wyatt, I think she wants to leave quietly. Some people still believe she plotted to murder her husband. I doubt Kevin Wyatt has much of a future with the bank either because of his involvement with Ferguson. Thank goodness for Ellen Ferguson alerting us to their plan."

Anna shook her head. "It's a shame, really. Adele allowed greed to control her."

"You know, I really thought Kevin Wyatt had killed Donald Dickson. I was so wrong. He was only guilty of scheming with Ferguson."

Chuck chimed in, "I heard she and Wyatt dissolved their partnership. Wyatt dreamed of getting rich quick by tying his fortunes to Adele and her family's money. Nope... that bubble burst along with the mining deal— bad news from the start."

I nodded, thinking of how close we had come to losing part of Meadowood to fracking, all for the sake of money. "At least that chapter is over. Now we can focus on the future."

"Speaking of the future," Fran said, joining us with a plate full of cake. "I've got plans for this town. Big ones."

"What kind of plans?" Colleen asked, her curiosity piqued.

"Well, for starters," Fran said between bites of cake, "I want to make

Meadowood a hub for small businesses. We've got so much potential here, and we need to support local entrepreneurs. And we need more spaces for the arts—galleries, theaters, you name it. We need to expand our tourism while preserving our heritage."

I could feel the excitement building in the air. Fran had always been a dreamer, but now, as mayor, she had the power to make those dreams come true.

"Count me in," I said with a grin. "As a partner of the A&M Tea Shop, I'm ready for whatever you've got planned."

We all laughed, but I could tell that everyone was on board with Fran's vision. The town was ready for a fresh start, and we had the right person leading the charge.

The evening wore on, with music playing softly in the background and the glow of lanterns casting a warm light over the party. It was a celebration not just of Fran's victory and the capture of a murderer, but of Meadowood itself—the town had weathered scandals, solved mysteries, and come out stronger on the other side.

As I stood there, surrounded by friends and family, I couldn't help but feel grateful. We had solved the mystery of Mayor Dickson's murder, avoided the danger of fracking, and now we were welcoming a new era for our town. And at the center of it all was my Aunt Fran, ready to take Meadowood to new heights. The future looked bright, and for the first time in a long while, I knew we were in good hands.

The stars twinkled overhead as Doug draped his arm around my shoulders and I clinked glasses with Anna, Colleen, and the rest of the gang. We had come through so much, but tonight was about celebrating —celebrating a town we loved and the people who made it special. And I couldn't wait to see what came next for all of us.

Author Biography

Now an award winning author, Nancy M. Wade challenged herself to finish the novel that had been started years earlier after she retired from the Dept. of Defense in 2012. The result one year later was _Endless Circle_. The first book in the Circle D Saga Trilogy.

Nancy and her husband are living their retirement dream in the hills of N.E. Tennessee. She's an active member of the Lost State Writer's Guild of the Tri-Cities area of TN/VA. Determined to complete another personal challenge and bucket list item, Nancy went back to school at the golden age of 69 to complete her Bachelor's of Science degree. Graduating in 2022 with Summa Cum Laude honors from East State Tennessee University, Nancy concentrated in criminology and film studies.

An avid lover of western movies and books, Nancy developed the Circle-D Saga — a western action adventure trilogy of love and hatred. The story begins in 1885 with _Endless Circle_ with three families then follows them during WWII in _Moment in Time_ and concludes with _Gun for Hire_ telling the tale of gunslinger Cody Jarvis and his connection in the saga.

Based upon her years of living in the mid-west, Nancy wrote a small town, cozy mystery series: *A Meadowood Mystery* that showcases the antics of amateur sleuth housewife, cub scout leader, and tea shop owner Meredith Gardner. Along with friends and family, she explores perilous situations to solve crime in six different novels.

Nancy's latest cozy mystery series is *A Maddie Brooke Mystery* with *Innvitation to Murder* – a ghostly cozy murder mystery set in the Magnolia Blossom Inn, a historic southern bed and breakfast inherited by young Maddie Brooke.

She is also the author of a rich family drama, *Reflections: A Sentimental Journey* inspired by the courtship and early married years of her parents; a colonial historical romance novel, *Frontier Heart*; and a contemporary short story called *Courtship of Laura.*

Follow Nancy on social media with both Instagram and on her author Facebook page. Discover her upcoming work on her web page plus excerpts of her writing.

Excerpt: Reunion with Death

Reunions are supposed to be fun and a time to celebrate memories and friendships, but not when murder and betrayal intrude as unwanted guests at the Meadowood High School 15-year Class Reunion. The victim is unknown to all but her killer. Who is she? What can Meredith Gardner do when her own husband becomes the prime suspect? Jealousy and passion clash with greed and betrayal. Can Meredith trust her former beau, Bryan Kirkland? The years have changed him; he's not the person she remembers. There's more at stake here than learning the identity of a dead woman.

Meredith (Merry) is a busy wife and mom who always finds time for community projects, leading a cub scout troop or taking care of her many Avon cosmetic customers. Her cheery, positive and can-do attitude carry her through dire circumstances; especially when dead bodies keep dropping on her doorstep. Merry once again enlists her Aunt Fran and friends to help solve this cozy mystery entangling past loves, a mysterious woman, fraud, and old classmates in their rural, mid-western town of Meadowood.

Excerpt: Deathly Wedding Woes

Meadowood in June means fragrant flowers, green lawns, and the ideal setting for the town's favorite school principle, Colleen Callahan, to wed hunky bachelor Ron Wythe. Friends, Merry and Anna, plan the perfect bridal shower in their quaint tea shop before the beautiful ceremony will be held at the lush Oak Meadow Inn. What could go wrong? How about a dead body found on the venue? Only in Meadowood could the ideal wedding suddenly develop deathly woes.

When Merry jumps into the fray to investigate she discovers more layers to the crime than the three-tier wedding cake, like the shocking truth that the groom has a twin brother and an estranged father he hasn't seen in years. Federal agents, big money and major fraud, plus underworld crime syndicates are too much for a small rural town like Meadowood, unless a determined amateur sleuth and her gal pals are on hand to find the truth and bring the villains to justice. Join the fun and follow the clues that lead love and friendship to restore Colleen's wedding from woeful to wonderful.

Excerpt: Berry Little Murder

Meadowood has a new mystery and it's just in time for the holidays!

Strings of miniature sparkling lights adorn tree branches and hang across the entrance to the holiday pavilion. Christmas carolers try to enhance the holiday mood, but it was murder in the air, not friendship and goodwill. What can Meredith Gardner (busy housewife, mother, cub scout den leader, and community activist) do when suddenly her new friend plus the local sheriff both collapse after drinking cups of poisoned mulled cider? Suspicion and fear run rampant in the town of Meadowood as local businesses are burglarized and everyone becomes a suspect. Newly promoted Chief Deputy Sheriff Doug Gardner butts head with his stubborn wife as she inserts herself into his murder investigation, risking her own life. With the help of her gal pals, Merry sets out to prove his prime suspect innocent while laying a trap for the serial robber and possible murderer too.

Christmas in Meadowood may never be the same again.